The F

By Chuck Cusimano

Artwork by Joe Milazzo, Minden, NV

The Foundling

by Chuck Cusimano

Copyright © 2019

All rights reserved

In no way is this story true to any known fact. Some of the places are real but many are made up for the sake of a good story. The characters are made up as well with no intentional resemblance to any persons, living or dead. This story is purely for entertainment purposes.

No part of this book may be reproduced or transmitted in any form or by any means, electronic or mechanical, including photocopying, recording or by any information storage or retrieval system without the permission of the author, Chuck Cusimano.

Table of Contents

The Foundling 2

About the Author 5

Acknowledgements 6

Forward 7

Cast of Characters 8

Chapter 1 10

Chapter 2 14

Chapter 3 17

Chapter 4 21

Chapter 5 28

Chapter 6 35

Chapter 7 39

Chapter 8 45

Chapter 9 55

Chapter 10 65

Chapter 11 72

Chapter 12 84

Chapter 13 93

Chapter 14 102

Chapter 15 115

Chapter 16 125

Chapter 17 133

Chapter 18 139

Chapter 19 144

About the Author

Born and raised in Southeastern Colorado in a ranching family in 1948, Chuck Cusimano grew up on working cattle ranches where his father was employed as a full-time cowboy.

Chuck's dad also played music so it was natural for a love for both vocations to play into Chuck Cusimano's future.

Chuck entered into the United States Navy in 1968 and served in Vietnam doing four west-pac cruises. He returned back to being a full-time ranch cowboy for a year and then began his career as a full-time Country Music entertainer. Writing fictional stories and his music was on his mind all this time.

Mixing cowboying and playing music sustained his living as time and opportunity permitted for many years. He's retired from cowboying now but still plays music. Being an Author is now a reality as well.

Acknowledgements

My Heartfelt Thanks going out to SO MANY wonderful folks who've been in my corner to get this first book in print! (Hopefully, the first of several).

There have been so many individuals who, through their encouragement and also their knowledge of "How to get it done". Many primary "Proofreaders" offered invaluable advice and suggestions as well as corrections about punctuation and protocol. Thank you!!

I fear if I tried to list everyone, I'd leave someone out but I certainly want to thank Oliver Davis (and Dolly) for taking the reins and constantly making the corrections needed to make this book a book to be proud of!!! Only with their help is this book a reality!!!

Thanks to many wonderful friends!! To have the friends I have makes me a very lucky man!!

I also want to personally thank Joe Milazzo of Minden, NV for the wonderful Cover Artwork. He can be reached at joe@milazzoartworks.com or (626) 321-6415.

Sincerely,

Chuck Cusimano

Forward

Lost and alone with only a faithful, lifesaving dog for a companion, a four-year old boy is wandering lost across the Texas plains. He is the sole heir to a nice sized ranch and all the cattle and livestock paid for, completely debt free and with a nice bank account. He is being sought by many people who would profit greatly by adopting him. The boy and his dog meet up with a man who has nothing and wants nothing except to see that the little boy is taken care of and wishes, himself, to remain lost to the outside world. The man knows nothing of the boy's inheritance.

Cast of Characters

The Foundling

    Timothy Ewing

Chapo

    Faithful companion

Adam Sanders & Tom Hale

    Cowboys for +I

Bill Blackthorn & Crusty O'Rourke

    Cowboys for +I

Jeremy Deaver

    Reclusive cave dweller

Ben, Margie, Troy, Iris & Ivey Ewing

    Ewing family

Granger & Charlie Ingraham

    Owners of +I

Bob Dove
> Saddle tramp

Nelie & Todd Sikes
> Sister and nephew to Bob Dove

Capt. Markus Lowe
> Texas Rangers Captain

Samuel Blair, Randal Sneed
> Texas Rangers

Ted Wills, Buckley, Fisk
> Texas Rangers

B. B. Kelley
> Cowboy turned bartender

Frank Jolly
> Wandering cowboy

Lieutenant Ford
> At Fort Belknap

Chapter 1

The sun was coming over the small hills to the east. Even a small child could cast a long shadow. The child making the shadow seemed to know that the other shadow had recently ceased to follow his own. Even at the age of four years the child felt the aloneness and emptiness. The eyes of the child searched far into the western horizon for movement. Soon the other shadow appeared beside his own and he felt the comfort and friendliness of the fur against his own bare legs. His hand reached out to touch the head of his companion. His companion quickly licked the boy's hands.

Traumatized from watching his parents and siblings being killed, the boy couldn't remember his companion's name or his own name for that matter. Just then, the boy realized that his companion was stopping him from continuing forward. The boy knew what his companion was asking of him. He lowered himself into the grass and rolled over on his back. His companion got on top of him and licked the boys face. The boy laid there for a while and rested. He was tired anyway and almost drifted off to sleep but he was aware of his companion omitting a quiet, low growl. Instinctively, the boy lay still. His companion was warning the small boy that a danger of some kind, was present. The pair had been wandering like this for four days and nights.

The day of the attack, Margie Ewing placed her youngest child behind the wood box to hide him from the warriors. The wood box had a wooden lid on the inside of the cabin and the box extended to the outside of the cabin wall. There was another wooden lid on it as well. The wood supply could be filled from the outside and used by those on the inside. When the fire became a threat to the boy, he crawled into the wood box from the inside and out the other side. The boy was now on the outside of the burning house.

The family dog saw him and saved the boy from being found by the Indians by pushing him down behind a wood pile and laying on top of him until the warriors left. After the Indians rode off, the dog urged the boy up and started guiding him away from the burning buildings and into the nearby water. It was shallow enough for them to cross without swimming.

The boy could hear voices but didn't know what they were saying. The voices were fairly close and the boy knew to stay quiet and still. In the recesses of his mind he could hear a woman's voice telling him to *"be still."* He spent a few minutes trying to remember who the woman was. Her voice, even in his memory, was familiar. The voice of someone he had heard even before he was born. He and his companion lay there, being still for a long time. His companion got up and left the grassy swale where they had rested. A minute later the boy also got up and went back on his unknown journey. His faithful companion, by his side.

Less than 50 yards away, Adam Sanders and Tom Hale were gathering cattle wearing the + I brand as they rode for their boss, Charlie Ingraham. The two were on the northwest quarter of the range and picking up a few strays belonging to the neighbors along the way. As long as a calf was branded or was still nursing milk from its branded mother, that was all the proof of ownership that was necessary. Everyone knew that getting caught trying to take one or altering the brand on one was a hanging offense. Cattle rustling was as frowned upon as was horse thieving.

Unknowingly, the two men had passed within a few yards of a lost four-year old boy. Timothy Ewing was believed to have possibly been taken by the Comanche who killed his parents, two older sisters and one much older brother. It was believed that the boy had been missing for four or five days with hopes of ever finding him alive gone up in smoke just like the smoke from his folk's burned-out home place. People talked about it freely.

Ben Ewing had made a nice home on the Salt Fork of the Brazos after returning from the war between the states. Ben was successful in everything he attempted. Ben and his oldest son, Troy worked well as a team and with the occasional use of a neighbor helping, they managed to put together and keep a nice, profitable outfit. Ben Ewing had made it known that he didn't owe anything in the sense of dollars to anyone. The Ewing land holdings and it's livestock was now sitting unprotected since the Indian massacre.

A neighbor spotted the smoke and went to investigate. He found the bodies of Ben, Margie, Troy, Iris and Ivey, mutilated in the yard. He didn't find the youngest, a four year old boy named Timothy.

With everyone dead, the place and its belongings, rightfully belonged to a missing four-year-old boy. The boy had an unusual birthmark on the left side of his face. It was a big red patch from the top of his head to his jawline. Some folks just had to talk and the unusual mark was widely talked about. The boy would be easy to identify. Of course, a lot of folks were looking for the boy so they could *adopt* him. They figured to take him in and eventually get what rightfully belonged to him.

Sanders and Hale reached the homeplace just at dusk and penned the cattle in the main corral for the night. Tomorrow they would sort the cattle.

Chapter 2

Jeremy Deaver had grown accustomed to living alone even before the war between the states was being talked about. His parents were dead and he had no brothers or sisters. He read his Bible and dry farmed the home place. Although it was small, it was all he had.

He was forty years old when he first heard that men and boys alike, in his part of the Palo Duro, were running off to join the Confederacy to fight the Yankees. He didn't want any part of their war. When the small troop of men gathering volunteers stopped by, Jeremy Deaver told the man in charge that he wanted no part of the fight.

Threatened that he would be shot as a traitor if he didn't join them at the forks of Mash creek and the Palo Duro the following Tuesday morning, Jeremy Deaver left his shack. He only took what he could carry and struck out afoot, heading for the caprock some one hundred miles south. He avoided all human contact and lived on what he could find.

He did have his father's cap and ball pistol along with powder and shot, a bullet mold and one lead bar. He had a good knife that he carried on his belt and he kept it sharp. He also had the Bible that his mother had used to teach him to read and learn his letters. He was a good shot but didn't want to make a lot of noise so he was careful to not fire the pistol.

His parents had both died and he didn't have much to leave behind except the few acres his ma and pa had squatted on. They were middle aged sharecroppers when Jeremy was born in Missouri and they struck out to find a place of their own. They wound up near the Palo Duro Canyon.

Jeremy Deaver walked on rocks for as long as he could and any time he could. He was careful to leave no easy trail for anyone to follow. He was wise in the ways of survival and knew which plants he could eat and which ones he needed to avoid. He was careful to not silhouette himself by staying to cover as much as possible. He caught fish with his hands in small streams and knew how to noodle the bigger catfish from the banks of rivers. He knew how to catch rabbits and rodents and would eat snakes if that was the best he could do. He ran coyotes away from dead animals when he found them and only took enough for himself. He was careful to hide any fires he made because he knew the glow of the fire and the smoke could be seen for miles and he did not want to be discovered.

Finally, he found the perfect place that he was hoping to find. This was the kind of secluded place where he wanted to build his house. The overhang was on the north side of a small canyon. He used a flat rock to dig the dirt in the back of the overhang to make the cave larger. There was a huge tree and other smaller trees that obscured the opening. He started carrying flat rocks and mixing mud and grass to put between the rocks, making a wall in front to enclose the cave. He positioned the opening in his rock wall on the side. That is where he would make a door by hanging a hide over the opening. Being on this side of the canyon, he would be protected from the north wind and he would receive the benefit of the sun in the winter. Winter came not long after he had his place ready. He had a decent supply of firewood but was careful to not gather any firewood from the vicinity near his cave. He would walk long distances to carry wood and buffalo chips to burn in his fire. He didn't want someone to see tell tale signs that there was anything suggesting any recent human activity nearby. Winter came and went then came again and went again. He'd tried to keep track of the seasons but finally questioned himself, *Why?*

Chapter 3

Granger Ingraham and his aging father, Charlie, owned the + I. The land covered several miles in all directions of the headquarters. Nearly a thousand head of native cattle wore their + I brand. The brand was first said as a joke during a poker game when a fancy gambler and two other men lost to Granger's dad. Two men lost money—but one man lost his ranch.

Charlie was still a young man when he started wearing a leather patch over his left eye. There were no doctors that could correct his eye that permanently looked at his nose. Charlie felt like the lord had dealt him a bad hand in life, but he tried to make the best of what he had.

He sat down at a poker game in Abilene and won the beginnings of his ranch from a novice poker player that didn't know a bottom deal when it happened. Apparently, no one else saw it either because no one was killed. Charlie Ingraham raked in the money on the table along with the piece of paper giving him title to the adobe house, barn, falling down corrals and *"as much land as you think you're big enough to hold"* when he laid down his hand of three jacks, Ace high. It was enough to start his fortune.

The fancily dressed gambler was jealous. but he suggested, "Since you've won a ranch, you need a brand."

Remembering that Charlie had lifted the patch over his left eye, revealing a crossed eye as Charlie scratched underneath the eye patch, the gambler finished by saying,

"How about the Cross I? it sounded like the "*Cross eye*"?" Everyone laughed, including Charlie Ingraham. Then the gambler drew it on a piece of paper. + I. That became the brand for Charlie Ingraham from that day forward.

The dust in the corral was thick from the cattle milling around as the cowboys worked to sort them according to the brands. The + I cattle that paired up, cow and her calf, were turned out and any stray cattle that could be identified would be held together in the corral until the owner could be notified. Usually, there would be a calf or more that had been kicked off by the mother. If that calf wasn't branded for positive proof of ownership, the +I brand would be placed on the left hip and turned out with the rest of the cattle belonging to the ranch. It proved to be profitable to work the cattle in your home corrals.

Several pairs wearing the – II brand were picked up on the south range and brought in with the cattle Adam Sanders and Tom Hale had picked up. The "*Bar Eleven*" belonged to neighboring rancher, Howard Tibbs that joined on the south side. Some wearing the / Y showed up in the west end's gather headed by Willy Bores. The *"Slash Y"* was owned by two brothers from southwest of Slayton Springs. They were known to *"Fight at the drop of a hat"* and they stayed drunk most of the time. Still, no one in his right mind would attempt to steal from them. Wendel Scott had the *lazy S* down south of Fort Raymond.

There were very few split rail fences built in this part of Texas and cattle had free range. It wasn't unusual to find cattle belonging to ranches from fifty miles away. In a case like that, word would get passed from rider to rider and then to several ranger stations and forts in the outlying area. The trading posts and ranger offices posted the notice outside their door or gave them to any law enforcement agents. Seldom did anyone claim the cattle. Probably because they didn't see the notice. The ranch that found the cattle would hold them and wait a while and if no one claimed them, the next calf the stray cow produced would end up wearing the brand of the host and every calf afterward. The unclaimed cow would eventually become old and die but if she produced a few calves for the hosting ranch, it was a fair trade for the grass she ate.

Noon chuck was called and the cowboys headed for the cook shack. This is where conversations would start up. Adam Sanders asked,

"Anybody hear anything about that Ewing boy? Has he been found yet?"

The feedback was that no one knew anything at this point. They all had their differences of opinion as to whether the boy was with the Comanche or if he would even still be alive. His body was the only one not found after the massacre. They even disagreed which side of the boy's face the birth mark was on.

Listening in was a saddle tramp named Bob Dove. Bob was a self-professed gunfighter, fist fighter and all-around bad man but he knew how to escape a showdown. He always had an excuse that kept him from proving how bad he was. He was temporary help at the + I. He would be gone within the month. To underestimate Bob Dove's scheming ways would not serve well and Granger Ingraham had figured that much out already. He was keeping an eye on the man.

Chapter 4

The boy and his companion traveled west until they came upon a high rim overlooking a canyon. The companion forced the boy down on the ground in a shady spot and stayed until the boy went to sleep in the shade of some cedar trees. The companion went off the rim to investigate something that caught his interest. The companion saw movement down by the live stream of water flowing below. The companion realized it was a human. This made the companion wary and he snuck in close to see what kind of a heart the strange man had.

By watching the human, the companion judged him to be a kind person. The companion would die before he would put the boy in harm's way, but he knew the boy needed food, water and attention to his health. The companion let himself be seen by the man. The man called the dog to come to him. Slowly, the dog inched his way toward the human. Soon the human reached out very carefully and touched the top of the dog's head. The human was being gentle and started petting the dog. The dog heard the man speaking to him,

"Where in the world did you come from?"

The fact the dog was here made the man a little jumpy. It was unlikely that the dog would be here by himself. The dog might be with someone horseback, working cattle nearby. The man made the decision to get back to his cave. He was happy enough being away from other humans. Jeremy Deaver took his freshly filled water sack and headed for his cave.

The dog watched the man disappear into the rocks and went back to his boy. The dog had enough trust that the man would have to help the boy get fed and nursed back to health. The boy was still sleeping so the dog curled up by him and slept as well. The dog woke up when the boy stirred. The boy stood up and let the dog lead him cautiously off the rim and down to the water.

On the way down, the distinct sound of a rattlesnake could be heard. It was loud enough in the stillness, from across the canyon, that Deaver could hear it. Jeremy Deaver saw the boy and the dog working their way off the rim of the canyon on the opposite side. He could see that the boy was worn out and possibly hurt. Jeremy Deaver instinctively wanted to go to the boy and help him but hesitated in case there were other people with the boy and dog. Before Deaver could move, the dog got in front of the boy and guided him away from the rattlesnake.

As Jeremy Deaver watched, hidden behind some brush on the other side of the canyon, the boy followed the dog. He could see that the boy was walking on sore feet. Deaver watched as the boy drank from the stream below and was impressed that the dog kept the boy from drinking too much at one time.

Deaver saw no other people with the boy and the dog. Twenty minutes or more passed as the dog let the boy slake his thirst. The dog started leading the boy to the cave house of Jeremy Deaver as if he knew exactly where it was.

Back at the + I ranch, Granger Ingraham and Adam Sanders were holding down an unbranded calf that wouldn't pair up with a prospective mother so, as was the custom, the + I was branded into the calf's hide. There weren't a lot of unbranded calves in this gather but the + I ranch did pick up a few that day. The branding was finished by mid afternoon and the crew headed to the bunk house to await supper. Conversation and smoke filled the room as many of the cowboys relaxed with their boots off. The usual card game was in full swing when the talk of the Ewing boy came up again.

Bob Dove was forming a plan as he listened to the talk about the lost boy with the birthmark on his face. He wanted to go visit his sister in the little town of Single Tree.

His sister's five-year-old son, Todd might be passed off for the Ewing boy with the help of some berry juice. He would take a ride that way as soon as he could draw his pay. He went to see Granger in the main house.

"Takin off on us, are ya Bob?" asked Ingraham.

Bob Dove said, "I need to go to Single Tree and see about my sister. She may need part of my wages to help her out of a tight spot."

Granger Ingraham told the man to wait in the parlor and went to the safe to get the man's thirty dollars. Dove hadn't been there a full month, but Ingraham decided to pay him the full month's wages. He was just a couple days shy. Granger paid the money to Bob Dove and the next morning, Bob Dove and his horse were gone.

Bob Dove rode into Single Tree and went to his sister's shack. His nephew was playing outside in the dirt. Bob spoke to the boy, but the dirty, scruffy boy paid him no attention. There was a man inside, putting his clothes back on when Bob pushed the door open. The man squeezed in between Bob and his sister Nelly as he made his exit. Bob was halfway blocking the doorway. The man said, "Gee-zus mister!? I guess it's *your* turn?!!"

Nelly Sikes was pulling her ragged robe together, holding a couple dollars in her hand, as she looked at her brother. She said, "Bob?! What in the hell do you want? I ain't got no money!"

Bob said, "Looks like you jest got paid. Or was that one on the house? It's come to this? Has it?"

Nelly Sikes said, "It hasn't been easy for us ever since Johnny got his self killed!"

Bob sat down and outlined his plan to his sister. He was going to borrow the boy, Todd. He planned to smear the boys face with some berry juice and see if he could pass him off as the Ewing boy to claim the Ewing spread. He told Nelly that he would have her join them later on the ranch if things worked out.

Back at the Yellow House rim, Jeremy Deaver watched the boy, following the faithful dog as they made the last few steps to Deaver's cave house. The boy startled when he first saw Deaver. The man was scraggly dressed in part cloth and part buckskin. The man was wild looking with his long hair and beard. The dog wasn't alarmed, and Timothy Ewing realized that his companion accepted this human as safe for them both. Deaver immediately recognized that the boy and the dog had to be hungry. He handed them each some food. The boy didn't pay any attention to the dirty hands of Jeremy Deaver. He ate the meat that the man gave him. Deaver looked at the boy and couldn't decide what was on the boy's face.

He asked the boy, "Who's your folks? Ya got a mama and daddy?"

The boy looked at Deaver like he didn't comprehend. Actually, The boy couldn't remember anything about his past. He waited until the man spoke again and shrugged his shoulders when the man repeated the question. Jeremy Deaver was looking at the boy's bleeding feet and noted the fact that the boy was covered in mud, dirt and even some blood. Deaver carried the boy back down to the running water in the bottom of the canyon. The dog followed along. Jeremy Deaver used moss from the creekbank to gently wash some of the filth off the boy. Some of the mud had caked in the boy's hair and it took a little more force to remove it. The boy didn't whimper or resist. Soon enough, Jeremy looked at the finished product and found a nice-looking little boy under all that dirt.

Deaver said, "You're not a bad lookin young'un with the dirt all washed off."

The boy drank some more water and followed Deaver back up to his cave.

When Jeremy Deaver tried talking to the boy, the dog would wag his tail, but the boy didn't respond. He coughed, he giggled when his dog would get playful with him, but he didn't say any words. He wouldn't answer any questions, he just sat there.

Night came and Jeremy fixed a bed of deer hides for his guests. The dog lay as close to the boy as he could get. Morning came and Jeremy fixed some more of the deer meat he had by cooking it over an open flame. He waited until it was cool before he let the boy have any. The boy ate till he was full and when Jeremy offered him some more, the boy shook his head as if to say "No." Jeremy Deaver read a few pages of the Bible he had brought with him and it appeared that the boy was listening.

Jeremy had never seen a birth mark like the one the boy had and he studied it. He wondered if the boy had been in some kind of accident or if, perhaps, the boy was born with it. Deaver had lived in this cave, undetected and hidden from the rest of society for seven years. He didn't know the war between the states was over. He didn't know that no one was looking for him. He was at least one hundred miles from the place he left on the Palo Duro.

When Jeremy spotted other humans, he stayed hidden and didn't make any tracks for a couple days. He would sometimes see men riding horses tending to cattle. He avoided Indians and white men alike. Jeremy knew how to trap and snare various animals. Some for food and some for furs. He knew how to use the thread from the yucca plant to sew and make his own clothes. He made a warm coat for the winters. He made his own moccasins and fur cap. He found uses for the raw hide from an occasional buffalo that he would find that was killed by predators.

There was a natural crack in the rocks at the top part of the cave where two rocks had fallen together. Above that crack were some cedar trees that helped break up any smoke that came from the small fire pit on the dirt floor of the cave near the entrance.

Jeremy Deaver made his own bow and his own arrows. Occasionally, he would pick up an arrowhead that was lost by someone long ago and by studying them, he figured out how to chip flakes off of the flint material that he found ample amounts of to make the tips for his willow arrows. At first the arrowheads were crude but in time Deaver became quite accomplished at making them. He learned patience and became a very good marksman with his bow. He still had powder and shot for his firearm but was saving it. He didn't know what he was saving it for, but he wasn't about to waste it and he sure didn't want to give away his secret hide out. He never knew when someone might hear the sound of a gunshot and come to investigate.

Chapter 5

Bob Dove stayed two days with his sister and her son Todd. He coached the boy to say that now his name was *Timothy* instead of Todd. He convinced the boy that he was four years old and big for his age. In reality, Todd Sikes was nearly six years old and he was big for his age. The boy could easily pass for seven or eight a lot closer than a four-year-old. Bob thought it was worth a chance. Bob and Nelly tried a few different native berries and smearing them on to the boy's face. It wasn't real convincing but then, neither one of them knew what the Ewing boy's birth mark looked like so it would be hard to compare.

Bob Dove wasn't sure where to take the boy to claim the Ewing ranch and he wasn't sure exactly where the ranch was. He knew he couldn't try it right here in Single Tree because his sister's boy had been seen in town.

Back at the Yellow House rim, Jeremy Deaver took his bow and his handmade quiver of arrows and went in search of game. He was a half mile from his cave house when he spotted two riders that would pass fairly close to where he was. He was good at concealing himself and took cover. The two horsebackers came within a few feet of him without ever knowing it. It was Adam Sanders and a man named Bill Blackburn.

He heard one man say, "Well. Whoever finds that boy, if he's still alive and not with the Indians, could end up mighty wealthy. That Ewing place is pretty dang big!"

The other rider said, "And all them cattle!? Money in the bank!? What's a four-year-old boy gone do with a place like that? He'll need a grown-up. A caretaker."

Jeremy listened to them till he couldn't hear them anymore. He left his place of concealment being very careful to not leave any footprints and went back on his hunt. He was keeping an eye out for any other people who might be moving around out here.

He figured the two men he saw were looking for cattle for one of the ranches in the area. He was also thinking about what the men were saying. Maybe the boy that the dog brought to his cave house was the boy the men were talking about. Jeremy guessed the boy might be about four years old and he sure was by himself, except for his faithful dog.

A short time later, Deaver heard a far-off gunshot. He guessed it was the two men he'd seen earlier. He decided, he'd check on the boy and then go see if he could find out what the two men had shot. If there was a fresh kill, the men might leave some behind. It would be dark before long and the men who shot would probably make camp. A fire glow would be fairly easy to spot out here at night.

Jeremy checked the boy and found him wide awake and hungry.

Deaver had started making some crude moccasins for the boy. He knew that the boy would soon be wearing them but for now, Jeremy wrapped the boy's feet in soft deer hide to protect them. Deaver had rubbed some deer fat on the boy's feet and it seemed to help. Jeremy fed the boy and dog some deer meat and they followed Jeremy to the water down below. After getting back to the cave, Deaver petted the dog and held the boy until the boy went back to sleep. The boy and dog had been here two days already.

Just before dark, Deaver left his cave and took his bow and arrows. He traveled quietly and quickly in the direction he saw the two men riding. Later he spotted the glow from the campfire he was looking for.

Adam Sanders and Bill Blackthorn had killed an antelope and were sitting back after having their fill of roasted antelope hind quarter. They were finishing the last of the coffee and talking. They didn't know anyone was within many miles distance. They were talking about their war experiences. Bill Blackthorn said,

"I mustered out in '65 and came to Texas after the war ended in early April. 'Course it was almost May before we got the word that Lee surrendered. At first, we couldn't believe it. We were still hearing some way off, far away shooting here and there. We finally run into some boys that told us the north had won. We didn't hardly believe that either! What about you Sanders?"

Adam Sanders said, "Oh, I fought with the First Texas Regiment. The *"Ragged Old First"* some called us. We fought in the battle of Antietam and the one at Gettysburg. I only thought I wanted to be a soldier. I found out pretty quick that bein shot at wasn't no fun!" There were so damn many blue bellies at Gettysburg, I almost pissed myself. I was lucky to get away without a scratch. By the second day of April, '65, I knew it was over for us. We were starving and wore plumb out. When I heard Lee was gonna surrender to Grant, I was layin sick in bed outside of Appomattox. Me and some others just wept when we heard the news."

Jeremy listened a while longer and then he heard one of the men say, "If I was to find the Ewing boy, raise him up like my own, I'd live pretty good the rest of my days."

Blackthorn said, "They say he's got a splotch on the side of his head. A birthmark. It's like he's branded or somethin."

Sanders said, "It's most likely the *Comanch* taken him during that raid. Or, he's died from starving. That was over a week ago. I don't recon I'll ever git rich findin him." Blackthorn said,

"If ya could find a kid that age with a big birthmark on his face, you could say he was that Ewing kid, whatever his name is, and claim the ranch, anyway couldn't you?"

Sanders thought a moment and said, "Yeah. I guess. Feller could go back east to some them orphanages and see if he could find one close enough to the description."

Blackthorn asked Adam Sanders, "What's that kid's first name? Anyway?

Sanders said, "*Timothy*. Timothy Ewing."

Deaver slept lightly in his hiding place only a few yards away from the two cowboys. He waited until the morning, when the two men saddled up and rode away at daylight. He watched the two horsebackers ride out of sight and then he went to the antelope carcass they had left. He cut some of the meat and most of the hide, rolled the meat inside the hide and started back to his cave. He would have some food for the boy and some bones for the boy's dog.

Jeremy Deaver was met just outside of the cave house by the dog who led him to the boy. Deaver got the fire going and started cooking a choice part of the antelope. He tried talking to the boy again by saying the name he'd heard the man mention.

"Timothy? Is that your name, *Timothy?*

The boy looked right at him and said. "Papa? Mama?"

Jeremy said, "No, little boy. I ain't your papa. Are you Timothy Ewing?"

The boy looked around the cave and said, again, "Papa. Go? Where Papa go?"

Jeremy didn't have an answer. He was unpracticed at holding a conversation especially with a four-year-old child. He took some of the meat off the fire and placed it on a piece of tanned deer skin on top of a flat rock near the flames. He took his knife and cut some of the meat. It was hot to his touch, so he blew on it before handing it to the boy. He said, "Here Timothy. Here's some meat."

The boy took it and started eating it although it was just half cooked. Jeremy told the boy that he could have some more after it cooked a little better. Deaver gave a piece to the dog that had a bone and the dog wagged his tail. As the meat cooked, Jeremy Deaver thought about what he'd heard last night listening to the two cowboys. A big birth mark on the side of the boy's face. That matched quite well with this youngster.

He repeated the boy's name, *"Timothy Ewing"*.

The next morning, Jeremy called to the boy, "Timothy? Are you hungry, Timothy?" The boy acted like he was familiar with that name. Deaver wanted to test his suspicions. Leaving the boy inside the cave Deaver went outside and waited a full minute. He called,

"Timothy? Come out here. Come here Timothy."

The boy and the dog came out at the same time. Jeremy said, "Go back inside ... Timothy."

The boy stood looking at Jeremy with a puzzled look for just a few seconds and turned around and pushed the hide away from the door entrance and went back inside with his dog following him.

This was a good indication that the boy's name was Timothy but Deaver wanted to test something else. He called, "Come out here boy."

The boy and the dog came out together. Deaver thought, at least the boy knows what *"come here"* means.

The boy's feet were still recovering from the abuse they had taken when he and his companion wandered from wherever they had come from to the cave of Jeremy Deaver. Walking barefoot, who knows how many miles, the boy had cuts and bruises along with a collection of cactus needles in his feet. Jeremy had taken care to try to heal the boy's feet with different plants and deer fat. His feet were some better but still sore. Deaver used some thick rawhide from a buffalo to make the soles and some deer skin for the tops to make a crude pair of moccasins for the boy. At least he wasn't barefoot now.

Deaver carried the boy to the water hole in the canyon bottom every day and let the boy soak his feet. Jeremy was still finding cactus thorns and pulling them out. Sometimes with his fingernails and sometimes with his teeth. He was committed to getting the boy healthy. After that, he didn't know what he would do.

Chapter 6

Word came to the Ingram ranch from a passer by that a small group of Texas Rangers had observed a band of Comanche that may have possibly been the bunch that attacked the Ewing place. It was believed they may have butchered the people and were suspected of stealing the small boy child called Timothy. The rangers watched through their field glasses for quite some time but saw no white child with them. The hunt for the missing Ewing boy was still on. Word also reached other areas.

Ranger Captain Marcus Lowe, from the ranger station at Slayton Springs, headed that division and he sent out rangers in pairs to see if they could find the boy or the boy's remains. Samuel Blair and Randle Sneed rode to the burned-out ruins of what had been the Ewing Headquarters to try again, to pick up any clues. Two weeks had passed and there had been a lot of folks trying to do the same thing, but Randle Sneed was an excellent tracker and maybe there was something that was overlooked.

Sneed found some footprints in the mud at the edge of the riverbank. They were the tracks of a barefoot child and with them were the tracks of a dog. The tracks led into the shallow fording of the river. On the other side, Sneed finally picked up the same footprints in the dried mud. The tracks were leading in a westerly direction. He lost the tracks, once out of the muddy part of the river's edge. Randle Sneed and Samuel Blair poured over the ground, ever so carefully and again found the prints in a now, dried puddle that was wet when the tracks were made. The pair of rangers kept at it until nightfall, made camp and resumed the mission the next day. Sneed mentally lined up the second prints with the ones found where the boy left the river and continued going in the line he was sure the boy was going.

Sneed built a small fire and piled some green brush on it to make smoke. Then he sent Blair out in front of him and directed him to move north or south by waving his arms. When he finally got Blair in the position he wanted him to be, Blair was lined up in the general direction Sneed figured the boy and dog were headed. Sneed used a point of high rocks for a landmark and the two men rode straight for it. Once reaching the point of rocks, the men found nothing, but Sneed used the smoke from his previous fire for a reference and picked out another, distant landmark to shoot for. The two men kept looking but didn't find anything that they were sure was evidence that the boy had passed this way.

The plan was laid, Bob Dove and his nephew would ride into the ranger station the morning after having camped outside a mile or so, the night before. Bob had smeared the berry juice on his nephew's face and was going to try to pass a big, five-year-old Todd Sikes off as the small four year old, Timothy Ewing. Dove kept telling the boy,

"Now, remember. You're Timothy. *Timm-ah-thee*.. Ewing. Ya don't have to say anything else."

Once arriving at the ranger station, Bob Dove and the boy were met by ranger Ted Wills. They were taken to the Captain's quarters.

Captain Lowe looked the boy over and said, "Mr. Dove, Please wait outside while I examine the boy."

Bob Dove questioned the Captain's suspicions. He argued, "They's no need for that! This *is the Ewing boy*!" He shouted, "I found him wandering across the prairie!"

Captain Lowe turned to ranger Wills and said, "Wills! Escort Mr. Dove, here outside and stay with him until I call him back."

Bob Dove told the ranger that he needed to go to the privy to relieve himself. When he got there, someone was occupying it, so he waited. While standing outside, two other rangers were walking by having a conversation. Bob Dove heard one of them talking about Fort Belknap wanting to buy some beef cattle.

Captain Lowe asked the boy to sit down. Looking at the boy in front of him, he thought a boy wandering around the prairies for over two weeks, with not much to eat sure wouldn't look this healthy. This boy was carrying a little fat and sure didn't look starved. The captain inspected the birthmark. There was something that didn't look right. The captain asked the boy, "What's your name son?"

The boy looked at the floor and said, quietly, "Timmo.. Uh.. Timu ..thee.."

Captain Lowe asked, "What is your last name?"

Once again, the boy looked down and quietly said, "Uh… Um, Wing?"

Capitan Lowe then asked the boy, "What's your mother's name? And your father's?"

The boy looked at the Captain and said, "Nelly Sikes. I ain't got no Pa. He's dead."

The Captain used a white cloth and some water and rubbed gently on the birthmark. The dried berry juice turned the white cloth a reddish-purple color.

The Captain yelled, "Wills!! Bring *MISTER DOVE* back in here! On the double!"

Chapter 7

One cool fall day, Jeremy Deaver was hunting again and was successful in getting a doe deer. She wasn't real big so after removing the entrails and keeping the heart and liver, he packed the rest of it back to his cave. The Ewing boy and his faithful dog had been with Deaver for almost a month. He had been fortunate enough to keep them sheltered from the elements and fed well enough. He saw great improvement in the boy's health. The boy's feet were well healed, and the boy seemed to be growing more comfortable with Deaver. The boy was talking better now. He'd answer yes or no. He responded to Timothy or Timmy, so Jeremy began calling him Timmy. Deaver read his Bible` aloud to Timmy almost every night and often told him stories.

That same night, Jeremy learned that the boy called the dog "Chapo." Chapo suddenly stood with his hair standing up on his back and emitted a low, soft growl. Jeremy quickly pulled the second hide over the door opening and put his finger by his nose, in front of his closed lips and gave a *shhh* sound. There was still some flame in the fire pit, and it gave off a glow inside the cave. They all stayed quiet for another half hour and Chapo relaxed as if to say the danger was past. After waiting another fifteen or twenty minutes, Deaver motioned for Timmy and Chapo to stay still then he quietly exited the cave and went into the darkness. Jeremy crept along the bench just below the rim and listened for any sounds. He heard the creak of saddle leather although it wasn't close by. He made his way toward the place he thought he'd heard the sound. It was very dark with the sun down and the moon not yet up and Deaver snuck along, picking his way, avoiding dry leaves, brush or cactus. He stopped to listen after half an hour and heard the familiar sound of a branch being broken. Probably for firewood. Someone was getting ready to make a camp.

Samuel Blair and Randle Sneed were stopping for the night. They had ridden the north rim of the Yellow House Canyon and were pitching a camp for the night. Blair said, "We might as well go back and tell Cap'n Lowe that we ain't found nothin."

Sneed said, "I sure thought I smelled smoke a couple hours back. And we found the guts and legs from a deer kill somebody made. And, it was real fresh!"

Blair said, "Probably some damn redskin." I'm getting tired of lookin! Tired of sleepin on the hard ground. We're near plumb out of coffee. We been out here, lookin two weeks or better!"

Sneed said, "Yeah, but. We find a track ever once in a while. I still believe the kid could be alive! Poor kid! Even though he's a young'un, he's gotta be missin his ma and Pa and his brother and sisters!"

Jeremy Deaver lay, not far away, listening to every word. He came close to stepping out and telling these men where the boy was. He felt that these men would able to help the boy get back to where he was supposed to be. He did hear that the boy had no living ma or pa and it sounded to him like the boy's brother and sisters were dead too. At the last minute, Deaver couldn't make himself give the boy to these men. He wasn't sure about them although his intuitions told him, these were good men. Jeremy still wasn't ready to face society. He'd lived by himself so long he felt he didn't need or want any other human contact.

Deaver snuck away from the two ranger's camp and went back to his cave. The next morning, Jeremy told Timmy about the two men. He asked, "Did I do right? Not telling them fellers about you? They sure are looking for you and I think a lot of folks are."

At the Slayton Springs Ranger Station, Captain Lowe stood in front of his office as he watched Bob Dove and the boy ride away. Lowe gave Dove quite a dressing down before making him and the boy leave. He couldn't do anything legally, because Dove hadn't actually broken any laws but he surly did question the man's scruples. There had been one other boy brought to the ranger station on Slayton Springs. The boy did have a birthmark, but it was very small and on the boy's chin, not the whole side of his face. Captain Lowe had two teams of rangers return after scouring the land for the missing boy. He still had a pair out. Blair and Sneed had not returned as of yet and it had been ten days and counting. Not a trace could be found, and the one bunch of Comanche didn't show signs of having a white child with them. The search could not go on much longer.

Randle Sneed and Samuel Blair were deciding whether to ride that north rim of the Yellow House again or just ride back to the Slayton Springs Station and report their findings. They chose to head back to the ranger station and call off the search. Had they decided to ride the ground they rode the day before they would have been approached by Jeremy Deaver where he would have turned over Timothy Ewing and the dog to them. Deaver watched all day to see if the men would come back. He had made the decision to let them take the boy back to civilization. He figured the boy needed a chance in life and Deaver didn't think he could offer Timmy much of a life.

Timmy and Chapo had become very attached to Deaver. After two months of being guests of Jeremy Deaver, the boy would curl up on Deaver's lap and lay there until he fell asleep. Deaver would hold the boy until his arms went numb and Timmy was sound asleep, then he would lay Timmy down on his bed of hides.

Winter hit and Timmy went with Jeremy to collect firewood. Chapo went everywhere Timmy went. Jeremy rigged a bundle and harness, tied a bushy branch to the back of it and hooked it to Chapo. Chapo would drag the bundle of firewood behind him and the brush that Deaver tied to the bundle would wipe out most of the drag marks. The three spent a lot of time hauling wood and buffalo chips to get them through the winter. Jeremy supplied the meat, taught Timmy which plants they could eat and although the food was the same every meal, they had enough to eat. Squirrel, rabbit, rat, deer, antelope and a very rare buffalo calf made up the meat.

One day, Deaver was looking at his reflection in the clear pool of water below the cave and decided to try to remove his long, scraggly beard and see if he could get the boy to help him cut his hair. Using some soap made from the root of a yucca plant and his very sharp knife, Jeremy shaved his beard. He cut himself a time or two but after a hard hour of scraping, he revealed his white face. Timmy was sitting there in tears not knowing what the man was doing, although he had blurred visions of his own father shaving. Deaver handed the boy the knife and asked, "Timmy, do you think you could cut my hair?"

Timmy shook his head *NO* and sat back further away from Deaver.

Deaver said, "You'd probably cut my ears off anyway. "

After rinsing his face in the cold water, Deaver took his knife and started cutting his own hair where he could reach it. Deaver would grab a handful of hair close to his scalp, leave enough room for the knife and cut next to his hand. Timmy looked at him strangely. Hunks of tangled hair were laying on the creek bank. Timmy felt his own hair and shook his head *NO*, telling Deaver that he didn't want a haircut. Jeremy laughed and said, "OK. But you need one too."

Chapter 8

Bob Dove took his nephew back to his sister and headed back to the ranch country he was familiar with. His plan about passing Todd Sikes off as Timothy Ewing failed but he hatched another plan. He would hide out, find a small box canyon and build a high brush corral. It should be easy enough to catch a few unbranded calves and apply his mark, hold them up in his hidden corral, get fifteen head or more together and sell them. Didn't he overhear someone saying at the ranger station, that they bought beef at Fort's Belknap, Richardson, Cooper, Chadbourne and Fort Colorado.

Dove found the place he was looking for and started building a crude fence blocking the entrance to a box canyon with some live water in it fed by a spring. He created a gate of sorts that could be drug into place. After a week of hard, sweaty work, Bob Dove decided, it was too much for one man. He needed a partner. He thought of two or three men that might fit the bill and started thinking of where he would have to go to find them. He would have to ride to Abilene. Bob knew he was going to need some supplies and he couldn't put it off. He rode out toward Abilene one crisp fall morning.

Meanwhile, Randle Sneed and Samuel Blair rode into the ranger station after being gone over two weeks. They were dusty and tired. Captain Lowe took the short version of their report and excused them to go get some food and sleep. They had orders to come see him after they rested some and give a full report. They enjoyed their meal and headed for their cots in the bunk house.

The Captain was drinking his third cup of coffee when the two men entered his office. Sneed and Blair felt some better, but both needed a bath, a shave and a change of clothes. The men had just come from their breakfast. Sneed said, "G'mornin Cap'n." Blair echoed, "Mornin Captain."

Captain Lowe said, "Good morning men. Are you feeling better? Are you ready to give me your report?"

Sneed said, "We did pick up the barefoot track of a child that was made in the mud and I'm guessin it was made about the time of the massacre. I'm sure it was the boy and he had a dog with him. The indication was, he was going in a westerly direction. We found another matching print at another small waterhole a couple miles away and lined up with where the Ewing ranch was. We kept to that general direction and didn't find any more tracks. We rode, *criss-cross* all over that country and finally come to Yellow House Canyon. We rode the rim on the north side and saw a sign here and there, like drag marks but no human tracks."

Blair chimed in, "We thought we smelled smoke, but it was faint. We found where somebody killed a deer and gutted it. They cut the legs off at the knees and hocks, but we couldn't find which direction they took the carcass. Probably, it was Indians."

The Captain thought about that for a minute and said, "Don't you think Indians would have left the legs on the deer to carry it?"

Sneed and Blair looked at each other and shrugged as if to say, *"Why didn't we think of that?"*

Captain Lowe said, "I think with as much time as has passed, the boy is most likely dead. But The evidence suggests that you take another look. Rest up today, get fresh horses tomorrow and go back to the rim of the Yellow House Canyon. Look for more clues there. Crawl every inch of that area where you say the deer was killed and you thought you smelled smoke."

Captain finished with, "Good luck men. Let's try one more time to find the boy."

Out on the Prairie, Bob Dove was glad to see the silhouette of Abilene in the distance. His throat was dry and he needed a drink. He could almost feel the whiskey going down his parched, dry throat like a horseshoe rasp. Maybe he should drink some water first. Just before dark he put his own horse up at the livery stable, not wanting to pay the extra ten cents to the hostler to do it for him. He didn't have much money and would need every penny.

He walked into the saloon, looked around and saw a place at the bar where he could stand without standing too close to anyone else. Once at the bar, the bartender came to see what the newcomer wanted. The bartender asked, "Whatcha need mister?"

Bob Dove said, "First thing I need is some water. Then I want some whiskey."

The bartender held a pitcher of water and was ready to pour some in a dingy glass and said,

"That's gone be a nickel. Whiskey is two bits. Let's see some money stranger."

Bob Dove found thirty cents and put it on the bar. He said,

"Kinda high, 'few ask me!"

The Bartender said, "We all gotta make a livin. Boss would fire me for sure, if I didn't collect the money first and I'd have to find another job. I'm done punchin somebody else's cows."

Bob Dove asked the bartender, "What's your name?"

The man said, "They call me B. B. Name's Billy Bob Kelly. Some call me Bob Kelly but, mostly I go by B. B."

The bartender asked, "What's your name?"

"Bob Dove. And, I just go by *Bob.*"

After the second round of whiskey, Bob called the bartender over again, he leaned in close, indicating he wanted to speak in a low volume. "B. B. Ya wanna throw in with me or do you *like* tendin' bar for somebody else?"

B. B. asked quietly, "What you up to?"

Bob Dove said, "I might know where we…you and I, since you said you know cattle, can pick up a few head of our own, put our mark on 'em and sell 'em to some of the Forts around here. These cattle wear no man's brand and it's all legal."

B. B. thought for just a few seconds and said, "I done a little time for doing something like that once, but," He paused, "I'm tired of tendin bar and it don't pay much."

B. B. was quiet for a few seconds then he said, "Let me think it over. I gotta go wait on that feller down at the other end. Hang on."

In the early morning hours, Sneed and Blair rode out of Slayton Springs just after daylight on fresh horses and leading one loaded with supplies. The Captain had made it plain he wanted these men to go over every inch of that place they talked about. It took three days, but they were now, within a half mile of the place where they thought they had smelled smoke. It was getting dark, so they found a good place to make camp.

Hiding in the brush was Jeremy Deaver. He'd been hunting when he spotted the two men a mile away. He wanted to know what they were up to. He snuck within listening distance as the two men made their fire and put their coffee pot on. Soon, the coffee was boiling and the smell was heavenly to Deaver who hadn't tasted coffee in years. He didn't miss it or think about it until he spied on white campers occasionally, who almost always had coffee.

Deaver listened to their idle chatter but he did pick up that they were Texas Rangers. He had to wait for quite a while before the men started talking about looking for the boy. He heard one of the men say, "Captain said, look at every inch of this country. This is where we start."

It was Randle Sneed who said it. Samuel Blair said, "I can't help but think that the Ewing boy has *got to be* dead. It's been going on too long. He should've been turned in by now. Somebody was bound to see him and being he's worth a lot of money, they'd know they could cash in by raising him and stayin at his ranch with him.

They could live out their years in comfort if they played their cards right."

Deaver thought about that. Jeremy Deaver didn't care a thing in the world about money. He didn't have any or hadn't even seen any since before he left his place on the Palo Duro. What he did care about was to see that the boy, Timmy was safe and had a chance to grow up happy. The boy sure acted like he was happy now. Jeremy had taken good care of him and saw to his needs as far as food. He even made the boy's clothes out of hides he tanned himself. The boy and his dog were always playing together. Jeremy read the Bible to the boy and now the boy was starting to talk like a normal child.

Randle Sneed said, "Tomorrow we'll get off this rim and search the bench below."

When Jeremy Deaver heard that, he made his decision. He sure didn't want to give up the boy so he would take Timmy, Chapo and what they could carry with them tonight and leave this place. He didn't want to be found. He went back to the cave and woke the boy up. He said, "Timmy, come on. You and Chapo and me. We got to leave this place. There's some men lookin and sooner or later they will find this place. I don't know, for sure whether they's good men or not, but we can't take the chance."

Within fifteen minutes, the three of them were gone. What they left behind would be evidence that someone had been living here. Deaver was a master at hiding his footprints by stepping lightly on rocks. Timmy had been taught to do so also. By daylight, the three of them were a couple miles away and moving carefully to not leave any tracks.

Samuel Blair and Randle Sneed planned to use the place they camped as a semi-permanent camp for now. They staked their horses and started afoot, checking ever so carefully the rim of the canyon. There were several places where they could get down to the first bench and they crept along, looking for any tracks or sign. They found occasional deer tracks and coyote tracks. Blair saw something that peaked his interest and he called to Sneed, "Rand! Come here. Look at this track."

Randle Sneed came but being careful to inspect the ground beneath him as he went. He was used to Blair calling him "Rand". He came to where his partner was waiting for him. There was a track of either a huge coyote, a wolf or a dog. They both knew that the boy had been traveling with a dog from some of the first tracks they'd found near the burned-out ranch headquarters. After discussing it, they both agreed, This was a dog track and it was fairly fresh. Now the hunt intensified.

Back in Abilene, Bob Dove and his new friend, B. B. Kelly sat in the back of the saloon talking in low tones about Dove's plans. Bob Dove drew the crude map of his work done so far and Kelly nodded his approval. B. B. asked, "Who's got some cattle close by?"

Bob Dove answered, "They's cattle scattered all over that territory. We'd have to do a lot of ridin. There's the + I, ya know? Ingraham's? There's Scott's *lazy S* and the - II, the / Y? Shoot! They's gotta be plenty of unbranded calves we could gather, but we gotta be careful leavin any sign and we can't afford to be seen."

B.B. Kelly said, "I got one problem. I ain't got a horse no more. I sold mine when I come to town here, a few months ago."

Bob Dove said, "Horses! Dang! We gotta get at least a couple horses apiece!" He paused and said, "I didn't think about that!"

B. B. asked, "You got any money?"

Bob Dove said, "I got a few dollars and that's it." He paused, "You got any?"

B. B. Kelly said, "I've got a little over thirty dollars saved up."

Dove said, "That aughtta get us a few supplies and you a horse. Might even have a little left over."

B. B, Kelly had a room in the back of the bar where he stayed. There wasn't a lot of room there, but he offered Bob Dove a place to spend the night if he didn't mind sleeping on the floor and covering up with a piece of tarp. Dove accepted Kelly's offer.

Chapter 9

Jeremy Deaver led his two friends quietly along the Yellow House creek bottom heading northeast. They traveled all night and into the morning. Deaver was guessing the two Texas rangers would search at least a full day and maybe more before they could stumble onto the cave hideaway. The men would have four different directions to choose from to start looking for tracks. Deaver was hoping for a full day to get ahead of them. He stayed out of open places and made sure to not leave any footprints. Jeremy knew the boy needed to rest so he found a place to make a dry, cold camp. No fire for them tonight and it was going to be cold. The three snuggled together in the half hide of a buffalo that Deaver had tanned. They had some dried meat, water and that was all.

The next morning, Deaver led his party onward. They came to Buffalo Springs and dodged any people who were in the vicinity. They snuck past a man filling some water barrels from the springs. They turned east and kept going. When three days had passed, the three fugitives, a man, a boy and a dog, were well away from the cave house they'd abandoned. They found a run-down shack of a house with no recent sign of life. They went inside and cleared some broken furniture out of the main room. There was a small metal stove that was comforting to see but the stove pipe was disconnected and the top part hanging from the ceiling. Jeremy soon had the pieces together and had built a fire. They stayed the night fairly warm for a change.

Timothy asked Jeremy, "Where are we going?"

Jeremy Deaver looked at the boy and shrugged his shoulders. He answered, "I don't know Timmy. I ain't sure what to do. I don't want to face any humans. I don't want to answer a lot of questions. But, I want to see that you get a chance to be something beside a runaway. Or a lost little boy. I know there's folks looking for you."

Jeremy found a root cellar the next day and it was pretty much intact. The door was heavy and stout. Deaver went inside and found some jars of fruit, some canned vegetables and some kind of stuff that Jeremy figured might be jam or jelly. Maybe it was still good. It was pretty snug here. There was a heavy quilt folded up on a shelf. It looked old and even though it was showing a lot of wear, it proved to be warm. It would be a good place to hide Timmy and Chapo if needed. Jeremy decided they would stay here for a while.

Randle Sneed and Samuel Blair hunted the bench under the rim, inch by inch and on the third day, they found the cave house. They studied it and decided that a grown person, most likely a man, a child and a dog had been living here for quite some time. The rock work appeared to be several years old, so it made sense that someone was living here, and the Ewing boy and his dog had found the place. They examined everything and anything left behind and agreed that the occupants had fled in a hurry. Probably because the grown up felt threatened. This could be a good indication that he or she was concerned for the child's safety. Now, came a problem. Which direction had they gone?

Before leaving Abilene, B. B. Kelly bought some supplies and had enough for two horses. He only had four dollars and thirty cents left. He quit his job and rode out with Bob Dove leading the way. Bob Dove only had his one old tired horse and was sure wanting to get at least one more for the tough riding that was going to have to be done.

It wasn't really unusual to see a few wild horses roaming the Texas countryside. They didn't belong to anyone and everyone was welcome to try to capture or catch one. There was a problem, a man could ruin a good saddle horse trying to catch a wild one. These wild ponies were fast, they knew the country and they didn't want to be caught. Bob Dove vowed to make a try on one if he had the opportunity.

The chance came unexpectedly when the men spotted a small band of *"mestenos"* as they were called by the Mexicans. The whites evolved the word into *Mustang* over a period of time.

Bob Dove shook out a loop and tried to single one out. The herd had scattered, and they were running in all different directions. Mares with colts were doing a pretty good job of staying together. Bob Dove took off after the closest one to him. He planned on roping one and breaking it to ride. It would be a lot of work and he may end up with a sorry animal that would be more work than it was worth, but he was out of options right now. His horse couldn't run fast enough to put Bob close enough to throw his rope and the mustang got away. B. B. Kelly had chased a different animal and was lucky enough to get his rope on a young mare. Bob Dove saw this and went to help Kelly with the situation. Bob Dove got his rope on the mare as well and between them they took a lot of the fight out of her. Bob Dove yelled to his partner, who was at the other end of the fight with the mare in the middle."

"Ya would have to catch a mare!" Then he laughed.

B. B. Kelly yelled back, "Hell! The bunch was mostly mares and colts anyway. At least she ain't got a colt by her side." Then he added, "The stud got away."

Bob Dove hollered, "Well ... She's got four legs and a back."

It took about thirty minutes of maneuvering to get the captured young mare to follow. The fact that she didn't have a colt with her could mean that she'd never had one or it could mean that she'd had one and something happened to it. She choked down a couple times before she stopped dragging her hind end, resisting their efforts. By the time they got to the brushy hideout, the mare was leading a little better. They estimated her to be about four or five years old. They staked her out away from grass or water. They would wait a couple days before giving her any of either.

Bob Dove said, "That'll soften her up."

It was a cruel method in some ways, but it had always proven effective. Starve them for water and feed for a few days and you become a hero to them when you do bring them some relief. Three days later, Bob Dove was able to get his hands on her. He used his saddle blanket to get her over being scared of him putting anything on her. Once she accepted his company and quit trying to kick or paw him, he eventually put his saddle on her. He used his lariat rope to tie up a hind foot to help keep her a little off balance, so she had to put some of her concentration on staying on her three feet. On the fifth day of captivity, she felt a human get on her.

Sneed and Blair scoured the countryside looking for any signs that might indicate which direction their prey had gone. They finally found a legible dog print near a small water hole. Whoever the grown up was, that was leading the boy was very good at concealing his trail. Sneed said as much.

"This guy knows his business. At least, I'm pretty sure that's the same dog track we saw that was with the boy when we found them foot prints at the burned-out Ewing place."

Blair said, "Yep! Six days to find one dog track that appears to be about five days old!"

Blair said after a few minutes, "Why we following them now, anyway? It appears the boy isn't in any danger."

Sneed answered, "The Captain wants us to find him, for one thing. For another thing, I want to find him and the fellow that's leading him."

Blair said, "Looks like they's follerin the Yellow House toward Buffalo Springs. Why not ride to Buffalo Springs and see what we can find there?"

Randle Sneed said, "That's some purty good thinkin', Pard."

They picked up the pace and two days later they were overlooking Buffalo Springs.

Jeremy Deaver caught a rabbit in his snare and cooked it for them to eat. It didn't appear that there was much cover for any larger game unless they might see a buffalo. He was always on the lookout for anything to eat. Water was the problem here. There wasn't any nearby, but Jeremy had found a small waterhole where a little tepid water seeped in. He walked the mile with his water bag he'd made out of a buffalo bladder, to fill it every day. It was just enough to keep them alive. Then came a light snow one night and when the sun started melting it, the run-off trickled off the roof. Jeremy caught what he could and saved it in a beat-up tin bucket he'd found laying out in the yard of this abandoned place.

Jeremy had let his beard and hair start growing back and had a couple inches growth since he shaved that one time in seven or eight years. His buckskins were dirty and greasy, and he'd left all the hides that he and his partners couldn't carry. He found a faded, cloth shirt in the root cellar that someone had apparently thrown away. He used his hands to spread it out and rub some of the wrinkles out. He tried it on, and it fit although it was a little tight.

A few days later, a bigger snowstorm came and gave them a couple inches of white, pure snow. Jeremy collected a bucket full and set it by the stove. After a while it melted into water. Jeremy searched for any containers to hold water. He found a couple of discarded bottles. After cleaning them out, he filled them with water and whittled a wooden stopper for them. On the tenth day they had been squatting in this abandon place, Jeremy spotted two riders headed his direction. Enough snow had melted in the hard-packed yard that tracks weren't easily identified. He took Timmy and Chapo to the root cellar and told them to hide. He waited to see what the two riders were up to.

Back on the prairie, Bob Dove had been working with this wild filly and the time had come for him to ride her. He wasn't proud that she was a female. Cowboys typically didn't like messing with mares. Although they could perform any task required of a saddle mount. Often times they had their nasty ways about them and were generally a lot more trouble than geldings. The filly had shown a little trust toward the men now that she'd been handled for a solid week.

Bob asked B. B. Kelly to stand by the entrance to dissuade the filly from getting through the flimsy brush fence. B. B. did as asked and took a wide stance in front of the makeshift gate. He took his hat off to wave it in the filly's face if need be.

Bob Dove used his neckerchief to place over the filly's eyes as a blindfold, stuck his foot in the left stirrup and had the headstall and reins in his left hand with the mare's head pulled back toward himself. This method was called, "*Cheeking.*" Now, he had the mare's left cheek turned toward his left shoulder, thus keeping the filly a little disadvantaged in her stance. He stepped aboard and set lightly in the saddle as his right foot found the right stirrup. Bob removed the blindfold and let go of the headstall but held his reins. The mare's first instinct was to try to rid the burden placed on her back. She wasn't used to carrying the weight of a rider and she didn't like the sensation of this human on her back.

The filly bucked and grunted and headed for the brush fence at the entrance of the box canyon. B. B. Kelly was right in the path of the wild bronc and rider as the filly was bucking hard with her head down and oblivious to where she was going. Kelly waved his hat at her, but she was headed straight for him. He jumped out of the way just in time to not get run over by her and her rider. Bob Dove was staying with her, whipping her with his rawhide quirt as she crashed through the flimsy fence. It was intended to bluff any animals that were captured but the bucking mare was oblivious to it when she crashed through it.

B.B. Kelly stood laughing and slapping his hat against his leg as he watched the bronc ride. His partner was staying in the saddle and the two of them were becoming smaller by the minute. B. B. set to fixing the brush fence. He knew they were going to have to build a stouter fence and a better gate. Kelly waited in the shade and pondered whether to get mounted and go look for the mare and rider. He still chuckled at the sight of the pair disappearing into the horizon headed south. Finally, he caught his mount and rode in the direction his partner was last seen headed.

Bob Dove had managed to stay in the saddle of the bronc he was riding although he'd lost and regained his right stirrup more than once. The scared filly finally broke into a run. Bob pulled on his left rein and eventually got the filly's head turned toward his left knee. This caused the mare to make a circle to the left and finally brought the mare to a standstill. She stood heaving and sweating. Dove could feel the filly's heart pounding next to his left foot. Bob was breathing hard as well but he was determined to stay on her out here a good mile from the hideout.

Thirty minutes later, as Bob Dove tried to get the filly to take a step, he spotted B. B. Kelly riding toward him. The filly had sulled up and didn't want to take a step. Bob kicked her and swatted her with his quirt, but she refused to cooperate. When Kelly rode up, the filly nickered to the horse B. B. was riding. Bob Dove had to smile, sitting there listening to Kelly laugh as he described the episode from his point of view, Kelly put his rope over the filly's head. After some persuasion, the filly started leading behind Kelly's mount, back toward the hideout and makeshift corral.

Chapter 10

Jeremy Deaver stood in the yard of the abandoned shack as the two riders rode up. One of the riders said, "Hello. Mister? Ya got any water?"

Deaver recognized the voice as one of the rangers he'd sat and listened to in the dark. He was full of respect for these men, thinking they had actually tracked him here from his cave house. He answered, "I got a little. I'll share it."

Deaver handed a bottle containing some of the melted snow water. The one who had spoke took a drink and passed the bottle to his partner. The first man spoke again. "Ya seen a little boy? And maybe he's got a dog with him. The boy may be in danger. He's traveling with an adult. Might be an Indian or a Mexican. We think it's a man, but it could be a woman."

Samuel Blair said, "It could be a Injun. Whoever it is, they know Injun ways. We found a bow and some errers."

Deaver rubbed his chin as he answered, "A boy? and a dog? With a Injun?"

The first man said, "Yeah. We found where he'd been livin with someone in a cave, down in the Yellow

House country. We tried to track 'em but lost all sign. We're headed back to Slayton Springs ranger station."

Deaver was careful to not let his gaze go toward the root cellar. He looked at the men and almost confessed that the boy was here with him, but he didn't want to give the boy up. He had grown very attached to Timmy. Jeremy asked, "So. Ya'all is Texas Rangers?"

The man doing the talking said, "Yes sir. I'm ranger Randle Sneed and this is ranger Samuel Blair."

Sneed paused and said, "Who are you? What's your name?"

Deaver thought quickly. Should he give his real name? Would it matter now that he didn't join the confederate army and fight the yankees? Finally, he decided to play it safe and give a false name.

"My name is ... Jerry - Jerry Tompson."

Sneed said, "Thank you for the water, Mister *Thompson*?"

The men started to ride away, and Sneed turned in his saddle. He said, "Mr. Thompson? If you do see that boy, He needs to get to either Fort Richardson or, better yet, Slayton Springs Ranger Station where you can ask for Captain Lowe and he'll take it from there."

Deaver and his guests stayed at the abandoned shack through the winter and into the spring when the green grass started showing. They had lived on whatever they could trap or catch in their hands. They stayed hungry most of the time. Deaver knew he was going to have to find a better place. He wanted to go back to his cave house, but he knew it had been discovered and by now everyone in the vicinity probably knew about it. Timmy was growing but he appeared he might not be getting proper nourishment.

Jeremy Deaver, Timmy and Chapo started walking east toward Fort Richardson. Deaver was going to take his chances with his past. He wanted to see if he and Timmy could stay together somehow. He was recalling something he'd overheard about Timothy Ewing being heir to a ranch with cattle and also, money in the bank. Jeremy didn't care about the money. He'd lived so many years without it. He only wanted the best for Timmy. If that meant he had to confess who he really was, then he would have to see what the authorities would do.

They had walked half a day when Deaver changed his mind about going to Fort Richardson. He was pretty sure he could trust the two Texas Rangers he had met and wanted to talk to the one named Sneed. They turned southwest and headed for Slayton Springs.

Bob Dove had been riding the wild filly for several months now, and between him and B. B. Kelly, They had only picked up a dozen or so, head of unbranded calves. They brought any of these calves to their hideout and branded them with a B reverse B. They used a cinch ring and some sticks to apply the brand. It wasn't easy work and more than once, B. B. Kelly said, "I think it would be easier to work for one of these outfits around here and draw wages than to work for ourselves."

Bob Dove said, "Yeah. But this way, ya ain't got no *BOSS* breathin down your neck!"

Kelly said, "Yeah, Ya gotta point there!"

The men had fixed up their hide out pretty well using the overhanging rock and some of the tarp they had left. It made a nice shelter from any storms and would keep them dry. It caused Bob Dove to say, "I been in a lot worse surroundings."

B. B. Kelly remembered his time in the territorial prison and said, "Yep! Me too."

The men worked hard every day and then one day they came across some cattle wearing the E 4 brand and it caused Bob Dove to think of the Ewing place that burned down and the boy that was missing. It gave him an Idea. He stopped his mount, swung his right leg over the saddle horn and said, "Kelly? You ever hear about that boy that was missing, sometime last summer?"

B. B. Kelly answered, "Nope. What about him?"

Dove said, "His pap owned these cattle branded the E 4 and his place over on the Salt Fork of the Brazos was paid off and money in the bank. It was said, the boy was the only survivor of the Injun attack."

B. B. Kelly said, "Oh yeah! I did hear something about that. But they was sayin, the Injuns took the boy."

Bob Dove said, "Well, Nobody ever knowed for sure what come of the boy."

Kelly said, so what become of the place? Who owns the cattle now?"

Bob Dove dismounted and said, "Looky here."

Bob drew in the dirt with a stick, an E 4. Then he took the stick and turned the E into a B by making the two connecting round marks in front of the E. Next, he turned the 4 into a crude reversed B.

He said, "They ain't nobody to claim these cattle!" We change the brands to ours and *WE* own 'em!!"

B. B. Kelly whistled. and said, "Damn Partner. I think it will work!"

Bob Dove said, "Not just that, but with the kid either dead or captured by the Injuns, they ain't nobody to claim the Ewing place. We could move in there!"

The pair schemed all night at their hideout and decided to take the cattle they had to Fort Richardson and sell them, get the money, move their camp and search for the Ewing place and any E 4 cattle they could find.

Captain Lowe had his rangers scattered around the country helping thwart the Indian problems that were popping up here and there. Randle Sneed and Samuel Blair happened, once again, to be near the rim of the yellow house cave they'd discovered when searching for the Ewing boy last fall and winter.

Sneed said, "I still wonder about that Ewing boy. I can't help but feel like he's still out there somewhere. I believe he's still with whoever or whatever lived in this cave."

Samuel Blair said, "Yeah, And I still think that raggedy homesteader, squatter, whatever he was, is the being that used to live here."

Randle Sneed said, "I kinda think you're right. His homemade buckskin breetches he had on? The tanning color matches some them hides we found in that cave, for sure!"

Blair said, "I still think we shoulda looked in that root cellar. Could've been, he was hidin that boy in there."

The two men discussed it quite a lot and told each other, if they ever got close to that squatter's place again, they were going to search for the boy.

Chapter 11

The funeral for Charlie Ingraham was a large turnout considering folks traveled long distances to get there. The buggies, wagons and saddle horses took up a lot of area in the Ingraham ranch yard. Granger Ingraham was sad about his father's death and although his father had been down in bed with coughing spells for over a week, the cause of his death was still somewhat of a mystery. The grave was dug in the family cemetery just south of the horse corral. Several neighbors came to assist in the digging of the grave and of course, some of the ranch hands did most of the hard digging.

Charlie Ingraham had always insisted he wanted to be buried beneath the big live oak tree there, so that is where Granger told the men to dig. Adam Sanders suggested, "Boss.? The digging there ain't gonna be easy. We gonna hit some big ole roots from that tree, I bet."

Granger Ingraham said, "That's where dad wanted to be buried so dig his grave right where I told you to."

Sanders said, "Okay Boss, I'll go get *Crusty* to sharpen a couple axes."

Crusty O'Rourke was the cook and general flunky around the Ingraham ranch. He was an Irish stowaway that snuck a ride to America in 1808 on a clipper ship that finally docked in Boston. Crusty's real name was *Thomas* but after working the docks in Boston, he arrived in Texas just after the war with Mexico was over. He had been wandering alone and lost when Charlie Ingraham found him, near death on the Texas plains over forty years ago. The Irishman needed a bath, a shave, some food and clothes so Charlie Ingraham took him on as an unpaid helper. Charlie started calling him "Crusty" and the name stuck.

Granger wasn't even born yet when Charlie took Crusty in, so Granger Ingraham had grown up his whole life with the man in it. Granger had heard the story many times how one day Crusty saved Charlie's life and nearly lost his own. The flash flood hit them while they were moving some cattle out of a dry arroyo, Charlie horseback and Crusty afoot. Crusty grabbed a stout branch and used it to fish Charlie Ingraham out of the flood waters.

Crusty was afraid of horses after being made to ride a bronc and the horse fell on Crusty's right leg, pinning the man under the bronc. When the bronc scrambled to his feet, Crusty was tromped on pretty bad as the horse got up. From that day on, Crusty didn't want any part of a horse.

Adam Sanders found Crusty cleaning up the cookshack and said, Crusty? When ya git time there, Sharpen a couple axes. Granger wants us to dig a grave under the big oak out there."

Crusty turned and looked at sanders and said, "Aye. It will be done Mr. Sanders. I'm going to miss me old friend, Charlie." He was the one saved me life…

Adam Sander noticed the tears glistening in the old man's eyes and said, "Yes sir. And I recall hearing that you saved Charlie's life too. "He paused and said, "Charlie Ingraham thought a lot of you too, old timer."

Just as Sanders predicted, they hit some huge roots that had to be chopped out as the grave was dug, six feet deep, four-foot-wide and seven feet long, allowing for the home-made coffin. Charlie's remains were lowered into the grave, words were said, dirt was thrown and three ranch hands stayed to cover the grave as Granger and his guests went to the main house to eat a variety of food and drink wine and whiskey.

Jeremy Deaver, Timmy and Chapo walked for days, avoiding any contact with people who were occasionally seen traveling one way or another. Timmy and Chapo had learned from their host to hide well and stay quiet. When they did camp for the night, Jeremy would decide if they could have a fire or not. The boy and his faithful dog didn't seem to care which decision was made. When the moon was bright enough, or if Jeremy could get positioned correctly, he would read aloud from his Bible. Timmy enjoyed hearing Jeremy's voice, but it usually made him sleepy. Timmy was talking more now and slowly remembering certain things. Jeremy would point to the letters and have Timmy sound them out. He was teaching the boy to read.

One night on the trail to Slayton Springs, Timothy Ewing dreamed about the Indian attack. He could see the many warrior's, painted faces and painted up ponies running into and around the ranch yard. He could see his daddy fighting one warrior that was grabbing his mother's dress and pulling her to him. Then he plainly saw his father get hit from behind with a heavy war club and his father falling to the ground blood spewing from the back of his neck and covering the ground. He could hear his mother screaming as three or four braves piled on top of her and were ripping her clothes off.

He had hidden where his mother first put him, in the far, dark corner of the house by the wood box. He knew the wood box lid could be lifted and there was a hole in the wall where firewood could be transferred into the inside wood box from the outside. Timothy remembered crawling through the wood box to the outside as the fire inside the house intensified and was getting closer to him. He remembered Chapo hitting him and knocking him behind the wood pile and laying on top of him. Timothy could hear the screams of his two half grown sisters and also the cursing of his older brother. The warriors tortured the oldest boy and eventually killed him. Then they left as the place was burning. Chapo forced the boy out into the water and across the creek thus, saving his life.

Timmy woke up screaming and it scared Jeremy awake.

"What's wrong Timmy?" Asked Jeremy.

Timmy started crying and hugging Jeremy so tight that Deaver was awed by the strength in the youngster's arms. Jeremy said,

"There, There, Timmy… It was just a bad dream I recon."

Neither got any sleep the rest of that night so before daylight, the three were back on their way to Slayton Springs.

After nearly two weeks, they came across an area overlooking a meadow with a stand of oak trees nearby. Jeremy went down into it first, leaving Timmy and Chapo hidden on the ridge. Jeremy could see the remains of a wagon there with a broken wheel. Someone had started building a cabin, it appeared. There was no evidence of people anywhere and Jeremy signaled for the boy and dog to, '*come on.*' Once they got into the edge of the meadow, they set up a camp near the wagon. Jeremy checked the wagon and found a pick and shovel. Also, there was some rusty tools, an old trunk with a variety of personal items. There was a rifle and a small can stashed under the seat of the wagon, wrapped in a heavy canvas like material, then the rifle and ammunition was wrapped in an oilskin thus protecting it from the elements. It was in perfect working order.

He checked all around for recent signs of activity but found none immediately. The way Deaver figured it someone had abandoned the plans to build here, leaving the wagon. They either didn't think it was worth coming back for or they were dead. There was no harness nearby, so whoever it was must have taken the team and rode to civilization somewhere.

The tools were still useable. A smaller camp axe and a double bitted axe, a bucksaw and a brace and bit set. When Jeremy opened the lid to the can, he found several gold coins. It made him wonder why someone didn't take the can with the gold coins. He would have to search a wider area. Although the weather was fairly warm, he used the old fire pit for the comfort of a fire, and they all went to sleep.

Deaver started searching the surrounding area the next day and came across the missing harness piled up on a log more than a hundred yards into the wooded area. He kept searching the area and found a skeleton of a human with another axe laying close by. Apparently, whoever this dead person was, was trying to chop an oak limb to repair his broken spokes in his wheel.

It looked like the man had accidentally cut his left foot nearly off and had probably bled to death. It was surly an accident and a shame the man had died. The man's clothes had been ripped away by predators, either wolves or coyotes or both as they started getting to the flesh of the man. Judging by the remains, this had happened at least a year or more in the past. The man's work shoes were there as well and although the leather had started to curl up and the left one had a bad gash in the top, Jeremy kept them. He spent many a night rubbing deer fat and any other animal fat he could get into the leather. He did a fair job of patching the cut in the left shoe. They were a decent fit and were better than his moccasins to work in.

Deaver had searched the remains of the man's clothes to see if the pockets held any clues. There, he found another gold coin and there was a crinkled letter in the pants pocket that had been wet and dried many times. The ink had spread to where only a few words were legible. The name couldn't be made out and only a few words. The best Jeremy could come up with was, *"See you before the snow."* That must mean, whoever sent the letter was coming to meet this man. There was no way telling how old the letter was. Mail was a very rare thing.

Jeremy had dug a grave for the bones of the man who had owned the wagon and its contents. Timmy helped pick up some of the scattered bones and brought them to Jeremy. Deaver knew that some of the bones weren't human bones but belonged to some dead animal. He said nothing to Timmy about it, he just buried all the bones together.

After the second day here, Deaver started cutting the best straight oaks for logs to build onto the cabin and make a brush arbor. Jeremy sharpened the saw and both the axes and made some painful blisters on his hands doing so. Jeremy dug some post holes and cut six tall posts. He tamped them into the ground and added long, straight poles on top to frame a brush arbor over the fire pit. This is where they would sleep, cook and sit while the cabin was being built.

There were wild onions growing here and some kind of potatoes the man must have planted at some point. There was everything they needed to live here, so Jeremy decided he'd finish building the cabin and claim this piece of ground. He didn't know how far he was from a ranger station, settlement or a fort but he planned to use some of the gold coins to buy a few things if he ever got the chance. It had been many years since he'd tasted coffee. He didn't feel like he was doing anything bad if he used the gold he'd found here. The gold and the tools weren't going to do the unidentified dead man any good.

A month passed and the cabin was nearly completely built. The dead man had started building it into the side of a slight hill by digging back into the hill and using the dirt walls as the back and a portion of the sides. Jeremy lined the dirt walls with native rock and mud. He used logs to build the front part and the roof. He used the dirt that he dug out of the hill for chinking like he had when he built his cave house. He built the fireplace, hearth and chimney that sat against one side of the cabin out of flat rocks that he picked up and hauled by hand. After laying and fitting oak logs side by side for a roof, chinking was placed in between them and then chunks of sod were placed on top of the logs.

Timmy had helped as much as he could. He enjoyed mixing the dirt, water and grass to make mud for the chinking to go in between the logs and rocks. Camp meat wasn't a problem, there was small game and also deer. Jeremy made another bow and several arrows. The small creek that ran on the edge of the meadow had some catfish in it and Timmy liked to trap them with his hands. Chapo liked helping catch the fish but Jeremy taught Timmy about the pointy fins on the sides and top of the catfish. Chapo soon learned that he was not supposed to mess with the fish. There were some grouse and quail in the vicinity so there was a variety of meat they could eat. Vegetation grew all around the area and Jeremy knew which plants they could eat.

Bob Dove and B. B. Kelly drove the young cattle that they had picked up and had also branded the B reverse B to Fort Belknap, collected their money and went into the trading post to buy some whiskey and supplies. Lieutenant Ford came into the trading post looking for them. He asked, "That B reverse B your registered brand?"

Bob Dove spoke up, "Well … Naw sir. It ain't registered… We just made it up and want to use it for our mark."

Lt. Ford said, "Ya aughtta get it copied in the book as soon as possible." Then he asked, "Where is your ranch?"

Bob Dove said, "It's west of here more than a hunnert and some miles."

Bob Dove looked at B. B. Kelly who was looking at the Lieutenant.

The lieutenant looked at the two men and said, "Well, … Ya wanna bring some more cattle here, we can use 'em."

The Lieutenant turned and walked back outside. Dove and Kelly agreed to get a couple bottles of whiskey, get their supplies and get gone. Dove and Kelly had visited with the blacksmith in the fort and asked if they could get the blacksmith to forge a branding iron. The blacksmith said,

"Yeah… But it'll cost ya a dollar."

He took their order and made a B with a handle. After a half hour, the blacksmith handed the finished product to Bob Dove and asked if they needed a reverse B as well?

Bob held the iron, pressed it into the dirt making an impression in the ground and said, "No… We just turn it over and use it like this."

Dove pressed the iron in and it made the reverse B just as plain as the first mark. B. B. Kelly handed the dollar to the blacksmith.

They rode out of the fort before it was dark and didn't make camp till they were several miles from Fort Belknap. Bob Dove was nervous, but B. B. Kelly told him, "We ain't done nothin wrong... Them calves was all unbranded and most of 'em were weaned off their mama. It's all legal."

Bob Dove said, "It give me the willies when that officer come lookin for us in the tradin post."

"He just come in there to say the Army would buy more beef if we want to deliver 'em."

Four days later they were back in their hideout and only had a half bottle of the whiskey left that they'd bought. They slept and the next day they went prowling for more cattle to look through. Bob Dove was riding the wild filly and she was actually making a good attempt at getting along.

With the funeral over and things back to normal, Adam Sanders was made *Segundo* in charge of the ranch. Granger Ingraham left to go to San Antonio to settle some of the ranch's affairs since he was taking over his father's position. The men had noticed a change in Granger since Charlie had died. He was abrupt and gave stern looks at the men sometimes. When one of the men said something about the change, Adam Sanders defended his boss by saying,

"He's still sad and a little lost without Charlie making the decisions. He don't figger he can show any weakness. It's gonna take a while for him to figure out how to tell us what to do without barking his loud orders."

Adam sent a crew with shovels and picks to work on the river crossing down by the main trail. Every time a flood came, it changed the flow of the river by filling holes that were there in the past and creating new ones where none had been before. Sanders took six cowboys with him to ride the south end of the ranch holdings. They were still on the + I range when they came across a small bunch of cattle wearing the E 4 brand. Sanders knew they came from the Ewing place. It was a good forty miles north east of here. They were in good shape and all the calves with them were unbranded. Although the calves weren't still sucking their mothers, it was evident to any cow man that these calves rightly belonged to the cows wearing the E 4 brand.

Adam Sanders said, "Let's push 'em up this little draw for now. We'll come back this way, pick up the calves, drive 'em to the home corrals and put the + I on them."

Frank Jolly, one of the riders said, "Anybody can see them cows are the mothers of them calves. Them cows are E 4 cows!"

Sanders said, "Frank! You're drawin wages from the + I, not the E 4!! You ride for *this* ranch. I'm Segundo and I say, these calves ain't suckin any E 4 cows and these cows are on + I range!"

Frank Jolly shrugged his shoulders and said, "Okay! You're the BOSS!"

The cowboys herded the little bunch of cattle, a mile or more into the mouth of a small draw and after deciding to drive them a couple miles further into the draw, went back about their business. They rode south till it became nearly dark and then made camp. They checked water holes and inspected any cattle they saw the next day as they wandered on their way. They rode the last fifteen miles more to the Briar Creek boundary. They camped for the second night and rode the next day, checking water holes and cattle. Things looked to be as expected so they camped for the third night and the next morning they rode north, back toward the home place.

Frank Jolly was quiet around Adam Sanders and finally Sanders came to Frank and said, "The old instincts in the bovine, for the most part, is to mother a calf. Same as any mother. When the cow gets to feeling she's gonna have to raise another, new calf, she kicks the bigger, older calf off and saves her milk for the new calf."

Frank started to interrupt and Sanders said, "Hold on. Let me finish. Even if they'd been a judge from the court room with us, he'd have said, *"Them weaned calves could belong to anybody."* So, it's the practice in these parts, if we find an unbranded cow or a *unbranded* calf that don't *mother up* with a cow on our range, we can put our brand on 'em."

Chapter 12

Bob Dove and B. B. Kelly were headed back on their quest to find more unbranded calves and any E 4 cattle they could find. They had ridden eight or ten miles when they came into a draw and found seven cows and eight calves. The cows were all branded E 4 but the calves were unbranded. They felt exuberance like they had just found gold. They pushed the cattle out of the draw and started driving them toward their hideout. Clouds were forming in the west and the men knew there could be a much needed rain in the future.

After getting the cattle inside their brush corral, they unsaddled their horses and fixed a meal. They would let the cattle settle a while before trying to work them. The calves were big and had been weaned for well over a month. The two rested and eventually went to sleep. There came a heavy rain that night with a lot of thunder and lightning but Bob Dove and B. B. Kelly slept right through it, snug and dry in their camp.

Adam Sanders and his riders went into the draw four days after they had pushed the E 4 cattle into it. It was still wet and sloppy from last night's rain so there weren't any new, fresh tracks. There were no cattle to be found either. The men cursed under their breath with Sanders saying, "I guess we should've branded them calves soon as we found 'em. At least we could lay claim on 'em."

Adam Sanders wanted to find the cattle but he'd been gone too long and needed to get back to the headquarters. Granger Ingraham would be back by now. They were still more than ten miles from the home place. They rode into the headquarters after dark. Crusty got up and fixed them a meal at Sanders' request.

Bob Dove and B. B. Kelly worked hard to get the calves branded and then they went after the cows. When they got the first one tied down, B. B. Kelly said, "Hold on partner, I been thinkin… So far we ain't broke no laws that would get us hung, or at least a prison sentence, but if we change the brands on these cows, already branded with the E 4, we've taken a step we can't get back."

Bob Dove looked at his partner and asked, "Who's gonna know? There ain't nobody around here gonna see us.. And, besides.. Ain't nobody alive to claim 'em!"

Kelly said, "I recon you ain't never been to prison? Branding an unbranded calf that nobody can claim is one thing but if we get caught changing a brand, that's stealing. I guess you know that if you skin a cow and look at the brand from the other side, it's easy to see if the brand has been changed. That's a hangin offence if we get caught by a bunch of mad cowboys and it's prison time if we have to go to court. If that boy is still alive, he rightfully owns the cattle and the E 4 brand. I think I'm done bein a outlaw."

Bob Dove threw the hot branding iron down and said, "Hell! We don't know if that boy is alive and if he is, he's just a button! I bet he don't know his pap's brand!"

Kelly was sitting his horse with his rope around the hind feet of the cow they had down while Bob Dove's rope was tied to a stout post and around the cow's head and one front foot to keep her from choking. The cow was flat on her side. Bob Dove went to the cow and with a jerk up on the head rope, and his partner giving a tiny bit of slack, he drug the cow's head forward just enough for him to slacken the rope and take it off her. When the cow started to stand up, Kelly rode forward, giving slack in the heel rope and the cow stepped out of the loop.

Bob Dove thought about what his partner said. They hadn't crossed *that line* that might lead to a tall tree, a short rope and a bunch of angry cowboys. Bob Dove said, "I guess we can see how many calves we can find for now. We can always change the brands on those cows later if that kid don't get found. Ain't nobody gonna be lookin that close anyway."

The cows were turned out of the corral, still wearing their E 4 brands and unmolested. The two men didn't speak about it for several hours and it was plain to B. B. Kelly that his partner still wasn't happy. Finally, the next day things were back to normal and the men were happy to have eight calves branded with the B reverse B. One month later, they drove the calves toward Fort Belknap to sell them.

Back at the + I, Adam Sanders was telling Granger Ingraham about the ride he and the men had been on. His boss listened and was happy to hear about the good rain that fell. Granger told about his trip to San Antonio and how he wished he'd been riding with the crew instead of dealing with a lawyer. Sanders told about the E 4 cattle they ran across and how they planned to claim the calves that were with them. Ingraham asked why they didn't, and Sanders explained that by the time he and the riders got back to where they had left the cattle, the cattle had drifted off.

Granger Ingraham told Adam Sanders, "Damn it! Them cattle are eatin *my* grass on *my* place. Getting those calves is just payment to me for them being here!"

Ingraham instructed Sanders to take a few cowboys and go back to that area and see if they could find more E 4 cattle. He said, "With nobody tending to the Ewing cattle, there's got to be a bunch of unbranded calves. I want you to find all you can!"

Randle Sneed and Samuel Blair were near the place where they had come upon that shaggy character where they thought the Ewing boy may have been hiding last winter. Sneed wanted to ride over to the place and have a look. The two men found the place and it was abandoned. According to the lack of tracks, it had been quite a while since anyone had been around. Blair went to the root cellar door, opened it and looked inside. He said, "Come look at this, Rand. This sure could've hidden that boy and a dog."

This gave them some hope that the boy was still alive. They still didn't know if the boy was in possible danger. The man calling himself Jerry Thompson might not be a good Samaritan and looking after the boy. They just didn't know. They were going to keep a sharp look out for Jerry Thompson.

Jeremy Deaver had looked through the dead man's belongings and found several items. Among them was a razor a brush and a small portion of a bar of shaving soap. After sharpening the razor, Jeremy heated some water, made a lather and once again removed his beard and crudely cut his hair. Timmy watched the whole process in awe. He vaguely remembered his dad shaving and his mother cut his dad's hair as well as his brother's and his.

Jeremy rinsed his face and looked into the clear pool of water. He rubbed his face and hardly recognized himself. He looked much younger and thinner.

The cabin was snug and cozy all through the winter and now that it was mid-summer, It was cool inside up against the back part of the cabin. The surrounding area provided game and just about anything they needed. Timmy was still growing and was seldom idle. He was learning to read and learning his numbers. He had plenty of energy and loved to play with Chapo. Jeremy worked and never worried about Timmy as long as Chapo was with him.

One day Jeremy spotted a couple riders, leading another horse, riding down into the meadow. They were still a ways off and Jeremy told Timmy and Chapo to hide and to stay hidden. The pair went into the thick stand of oaks and did as requested. The riders came on as Jeremy stood by the broken wheel wagon. Deaver never wore a gun although he still had his father's cap and ball Navy Colt put away.

He greeted the men as they rode up. "Hello. Get down and have some water. That's all I can offer."

One of the men said,

"Thanks ... We could use a drink."

The man dismounted and said, "Ya ain't got anything else?"

The other one said, as he dismounted, "Yeah. Like whiskey or even coffee?"

Deaver answered, "Nope. Ain't got nary a one of them. Just water, but it's good water."

The first one that had spoken said, "My name is Billy Bob Kelly, this here's my partner, Bob Dove."

Jeremy introduced himself as Jerry Deaver as the men shook hands. It was the first time Jeremy had shaken hands with anyone in more years than he could remember. The three men sat on stumps under the shade of a big oak tree for thirty minutes or more drinking water and visiting.

Jeremy wanted to ask about the war he had dodged but didn't know how to bring it up. Finally, it came to him. He asked, "Either one a you fellers done any soldierin'?"

Bob Dove said, "Naw ... Not me. I had a brother that went and fought the yanks.. He come back with half his leg blowed off."

B. B. Kelly answered, "I was with the First Texas outfit for nearly a year... Then, the war was over. I'm sorry we lost but I hadn't missed all that noise from them yankee cannons!"

B. B. Kelly asked, "How 'bout you? Don't tell me you was a *yankee*? ..!"

Jeremy said, "No. Guess I was too old."

Bob Dove asked, "What you doin' here? Are ya prospectin?"

Jeremy lied, "Naw. Wagon broke down and I liked this spot, so I built a cabin and just live here. There ain't nothin 'round here to be prospecting for."

Bob Dove asked, "What do you use for money?"

Jeremy chuckled and said, "I haven't seen any money for years and ain't go no place to spend it if I had any."

Bob Dove said, "They's a settlement with a tradin post about ten, twelve miles from here, due north. It's called, *Chinook Springs*."

B. B. Kelly said, "Yeah. That's where we're goin now." If ya had some money, we'd bring ya back some whiskey."

Jeremy said, "Well ... I wouldn't care anything about whiskey but If I had some money, I'd sure admire some coffee. I run outta them beans a long time ago. All I got's a grinder."

The men mounted their horses, thanked Jeremy for his kindness and rode out of the meadow. Deaver waited another half hour before he called out to Timmy.

Bob Dove and B. B. Kelly discussed the shabby dressed old squatter they encountered as they rode toward Chinook Springs Station and complimented the fact that whoever built the place sure knew what they were doing. They agreed that the old guy had a nice little place. B. B. Kelly said, "We aughtta get some coffee beans and take em to that old timer on our way back. I got a couple extra dollars."

Bob Dove said, "That old guy has done without for so long, he don't need nothin. 'sides, we ain't comin back that way. We're gonna find that Ewing place and if they ain't nobody livin there, we're gonna move in."

Kelly said, "I heard that house got burnt up by the Injuns. What if there ain't no place to live there?"

Bob Dove said, "Oh... There'll be some kinda somethin. I bet we can throw somethin together."

Kelly asked, "Ya mean just squat on that place? Fix it up and act like it's ours?"

Dove answered, "Yep... The only one that's got a claim on the place is a four or five-year-old, lost, little boy. A little boy that might not even be alive."

The men rode into the few scattered buildings of Chinook Springs Station and trading post. They would do a lot of listening and not much talking.

Adam Sanders and four other riders went back to the area where the E 4 cattle had been spotted and rode a lot of country. They took with them, the wagon and some provisions to stay out a while. They camped in the mouth of that little draw where there was a small waterhole. Adam Sanders outlined the plan to search for any and all E 4 cattle and especially the ones with unbranded calves. If the rumored word was correct, Ben Ewing owned near eight or nine hundred head of mother cows and it was rumored that he kept some of the best bulls in the country. Frank Jolly was one of the men on this roundup.

He asked Sanders, "What's the boss want us to gather the E 4 cows for? Does he want us to drive 'em to the headquarters?"

Adam Sanders said, "That's exactly what he wants. See, we can brand any of the unbranded calves from this year. Ya know they's pretty big now and then their mamas gonna have another calf pretty soon and with no one to claim them, we can brand the + I on those calves when they wean off next year. In the meantime, we got 'em close to home so some other outfit don't get the chance to do the same thing."

Frank Jolly said, "It just don't seem right to me some way ... I mean, that Ewing, he owned them cows and their calves and" ...

"They can't be owned by a *dead man*. Ewing is *dead*!"

Chapter 13

Jeremy Deaver put things away, out of the reach of any weather, took only a couple of the gold coins and sat Timmy down. He said,

"Timmy, I been tryin the best way to figger this… I want to see if we can find that trading post over at Chinook Springs them fellers was talking about. They said it's north of here and only ten or so miles. So, you and Chapo got to go with me becourse, I cain't leave you here by yourselves. Now I know they's probably still some folks a lookin for ya but I gotta be careful who I let know that you's still alive. So, we travel together, jest like always, but I hide you out when I see somebody else or when we git to that tradin post. I'll go in and git our supplies we need and then we come back here."

The next morning, just before dawn, the three of them headed out for Chinook Springs Station. It took two days, traveling cautiously and they didn't see any other travelers. Deaver made a wise decision by staying out of where the buildings were and having a cold camp the night they came upon the little town. It was plenty warm that time of year and they slept comfortably knowing Chapo had the best ears of them all. The sun rose the next morning and Jeremy Deaver cut a piece of jerky for each of his traveling companions. He trusted them to remain hidden here until he returned.

Deaver crept along the small creekbank until he could see the buildings and anything that was going on.

The first two men he saw were the two men that came by his place a few days earlier. Jeremy went back to where the boy and dog were waiting. Jeremy said,

"We gotta wait till them fellers leave. I don't want 'em to see me. They got horses so they can travel faster than we can afoot and if they wanted to go to our place, they could get there before we could. No tellin what they might do."

Two days later Deaver was watching as the two men rode away. Jeremy waited another half hour before he went to the trading post. Inside, he found some folded pants and shirts. He bought two pair of pants and three shirts for himself. It would be the first time he had new; store bought clothes for nearly ten years. He also bought coffee beans, pinto beans, flour, salt pork, sugar and a cast iron skillet.

He carried the things back to where Timmy and Chapo waited. Deaver scraped the weeks growth of whiskers off and cut his hair with his knife. He always kept his knife razor sharp. Jeremy cut Timmy's hair as well. The next day Jeremy made another trip to the trading post and found the smallest shirt and pair of pants that he could find. The three started back to the cabin by the meadow. It was awkward for Jeremy to carry everything even with Timmy helping.

Bob Dove and B. B. Kelly rode in the direction they'd been told by the man at the trading post till they found the burned-out ruins of the Ewing ranch. Judging by the tracks, this place was visited quite often. They were surprised to find no one there. They unloaded the provisions they had bought that the extra mount had been packing, tied their horses and made a quick camp. They noticed the five graves of the Ewing family. B. B. Kelly had a chill come over him as he looked at the graves that must be of the small children. He said,

Bob? This place gives me the willies."

Bob Dove said,

"We ain't gotta worry about nothin. Too bad these folks got kilt, but they did and they ain't nobody to run us off."

They sifted through the ashes of the burned ranch house, but other people had been here before them. They found nothing of value, but they started sorting out any timbers or lumber that may be useful for their plans. Using their horses and a big heavy timber, they drug an area clean for a place for them to start building their shack to show improvements on the unclaimed place. They were in hopes of staking a claim on the property. They had found a shovel that needed a handle. It had been burned in the fire. They found other tools that they could use but many needed handles. B. B. Kelly attended to the task of making handles for everything. The tool shed that these tools were found in had only burned about half-way, so some were useful as they were.

A week later, two tired cowpunchers were staying in a shack although they were cooking on the ground outside. Bob Dove said,

"Tomorrow, we start looking for cattle. E 4 cattle."

Kelly agreed,

"They gotta have some nice calves on them like them others we found."

Jeremy Deaver, Timmy and Chapo got back to the cabin in the meadow and nothing had been bothered. Deaver cooked some of the salt pork in the cast Iron skillet. He ground some coffee beans and set a can of water on the fire to boil. It would be the first coffee he'd tasted in many years. When the coffee was poured into the one tin cup they had, Jeremy put some sugar in it and used a stick to stir. He remembered his dad liked sugar and milk in his coffee but there was no milk cow around here, so he'd be happy with just the sugar. The cup was hot, but Jeremy used a piece of deerskin to hold the cup with both hands and sit looking into the fire. He felt like he was on top of the world.

When Timmy had a chance to taste the coffee after it had cooled enough, he sat right next to Jeremy and leaned against him. It brought a great feeling that Jeremy hadn't felt since he was a small boy when he himself sat next to his mother or father like that. Timmy had started calling Jeremy *"Dad"* not long after he came to live with him. At first, he tried to tell the boy that he wasn't his dad. He came to love the word coming from the boy now.

"Love." It was a feeling that Jeremy didn't even know he'd been missing all these years. He lived in that cave, shunning society and any other people. He had no human contact until the dog brought the boy to him.

Jeremy was thinking back to that day. He didn't want to be discovered. He didn't want to be seen by anyone. He only took care of the boy because he felt if he didn't, the boy would die. Jeremy became a man alone because he didn't want to fight in the war between the States. He didn't want to kill or be killed for any reason that he could not clearly see. Now, he had become attached to the boy he called Timmy. He wasn't going to give him up. He wasn't going to turn the boy over to an unknown fate. Jeremy started cutting and sewing on the pants and shirt he'd bought for Timmy.

Randle Sneed and Samuel Blair were riding from Fort Belknap to the Slayton Springs station when they came over a little rise and smelled smoke. They rode through the trees looking for the source. At the same time, Timmy and Chapo were exploring the wooded area behind the cabin and Chapo put his body against Timothy's legs and started pushing sideways. Timothy recognized his faithful companion's actions and went where the dog was pushing him. Timothy was older now, but he accepted the guidance that had saved his life in the past. Chapo pushed Timmy down in a low spot and laid on top of him.

Sneed spotted the cabin just before Blair called out,

"Look down there in the edge of the meadow."

Randle Sneed responded, "Yup. I see it."

The two men rode into the meadow as Jeremy Deaver stepped out of the cabin door. He surely must have looked different to these Texas Rangers since they'd seen him eight or nine months earlier. With his clean-shaven face, shorter hair and store-bought clothes they didn't recognize him. The two men had stopped their horses near the fire pit under the brush arbor. Sneed said,

"Mornin',... I'm Ranger Randle Sneed and this is Ranger Samuel Blair. Who are you?"

Sneed was looking all around as he spoke to see if there was anyone else, so he asked,

"You live here alone?"

Deaver said, "Mornin'... Uh ... Name's Deaver. You fellers want some coffee? I got the makins, poor as they are."

Blair stepped off his horse and said, "Ya got any water?"

Jeremy chuckled. He said, "I guess I better if I'm gonna make coffee."

Sneed dismounted and watched Deaver hand the only cup he had to the ranger named Blair. Deaver grinned and said, "They's the creek... Help yourself."

Randle Sneed asked, "You live here alone mister.... Mister ...?

Jeremy figured that these men didn't recognize him from that time on the wind-swept flats by that old abandoned shack. He answered,

"Yes, yes sir. I live here alone. My name is Jeremy Deaver. This cabin, that brush arbor, that broke down wagon, that's all I own. I can make you some coffee if ya want. I ain't got much else. I got a deer hangin up in the trees back yonder. I could slice off some meat and fry it if you like."

Randle Sneed said, "Naw... Thanks, but 'nother eighteen, twenty miles, we'll be at Slayton Springs. We got a nice soft bunk waitin for us there and some hot grub of some kind."

The men thanked Deaver for the water, mounted up and rode out west. Deaver watched them till they disappeared into the oak thicket. He wasn't worried about Timmy and Chapo being discovered. Jeremy trusted Chapo to look after the boy like he'd always done. The rangers talked as they rode, and they passed within fifteen feet of Chapo and Timothy in their hiding place and never knew it.

Timmy and Chapo came out of the timbers behind the cabin and found Jeremy frying meat for their supper. He told Timmy about the two men and Timmy said,

"We saw 'em. Chapo saw 'em first and we hid like you tell us to when we see somebody."

Jeremy said, "Good! Always hide from any people other than me."

Timmy asked,

"Dad? Did I do something bad? Is that why men's lookin for me?"

Jeremy hugged Timmy and said, "No … No Timmy. You didn't do nothing bad at all. There are people who want to take advantage of you."

Jeremy figured the boy didn't know what that meant so he tried to explain it.

"See. Your family was … Well, Uh.. Well … Your family, your ma and pa and them that was there with you. They, Th …they ain't there no more. So, you are the only one that, by rights, own that ranch and whoever has you can maybe get the ranch till you're old enough to take over as owner."

Jeremy continued after a short silence,

"I don't care nothin' about tryin' to get your ranch. I just want to see you get grown so it can be yours when you're ready."

Timmy asked,

"Where is … Mama, Papa and Troy? Where's Iris and Ivey?"

Jeremy didn't have any answers. He simply said,

"I hate to say, but, they's gone. They's not coming back. I 'spect they's in the house of the Lord."

Timmy looked straight at him and asked,

"Are they dead? Like when you kill a deer?"

Jeremy held his tears and as his throat tightened, he said,

"Timmy? Ya know when I shoot a deer, you know, I do that so we can eat. It says in the Bible, the Lord will provide. He made the animals so we could stay alive." When I kill a deer that's the end of it except we eat it. When God fearin' folks die, they live on, but in a different place. The Lord has a place up there. It's called Heaven."

He pointed into the sky, He said,

"And the only ones that can live there with him are them that gets saved."

Timmy looked up in the sky. There were a few small clouds floating like ships on the calm sea. He asked,

"Dad? Can we see 'em? Can we see heaven?"

Deaver answered,

"No Timmy. We can't see Heaven from here, but it's believed that when the time comes, we'll go there and then we'll see all the ones that went and left us here."

Night came and Jeremy finished the pants and shirt. Timmy put them on and was happy to be dressed like Jeremy. It wasn't long after that before sleep consumed the boy and the man while the dog kept a close watch on his people.

Chapter 14

Bob Dove and B. B. Kelly were checking for any cattle wearing the E 4 brand. They had fixed up the Ewing corrals well enough to hold some cattle if any could be found. They were thirty or more miles from the Ewing place when they spotted some other riders. They would have tried to hide but it was evident that the other riders had spotted them as well and were riding straight for them. Bob Dove said,

"I think I recognize the one in the lead."

"Who are they? Do you know just one?"

Bob Dove said,

"Pretty sure that's Adam Sanders on the dun horse in the lead. I even recognize his favorite horse. That guy on the blood bay might be Tom Hale. I think I see Shorty Meeks too."

By now, the riders were getting closer and Adam Sanders turned in his saddle and said,

Tom? … Ain't that Bob Dove?"

Randle Sneed and Samuel Blair rode into the ranger station just after dark and found enough grub to satisfy their hungry bellies. They went to the bunk house and crawled into their bunks, tired and grateful. Tomorrow, they would see the Captain.

Sneed gave his report with Blair standing right beside him. They didn't find any trace of recent activity at the flat land shack. No trace or word about a boy or a mountain man. That's what they had started calling the man they encountered in the abandoned shack last winter because the description fit so well. They talked to the Commanders at Fort Richardson, Fort Belknap and any travelers they came upon and no one knew anything. Sneed remembered to mention the man living alone, several miles east of here. He asked the Captain if anyone like that had been around the trading post.

"Ain't been nobody like that around here. What did he look like?"

Sneed said,

"He'll stand right at six foot, kinda lean. Clean shaved, reddish hair. That's about all I could say about him."

The Captain asked, "How was he dressed?"

Blair answered first, "He had on some new, store bought clothes, a hat, some heavy shoes, ya know? Like a farmer wears."

Captain Lowe said, "You men get some rest. And, go take a bath. Tomorrow, I'm taking a patrol to Abilene and I want you both to go with me."

Sneed and Blair went to the bath house and then returned to their bunks.

With a chill in the air, Fall was right around the corner and Jeremy started planning for winter. He went in search of firewood and with Timmy's help, they created a nice pile of dry logs only ten feet from the south wall of the cabin. The buck saw was right in front of it. There was also a stack of smaller pieces stacked on the north side of the cabin door.

Jeremy decided it was time to teach Timmy to hunt so he made a smaller bow and some arrows for the boy and started teaching him how to aim and release the arrow without swinging the bow until after the arrow had been fired. Jeremy had gathered up quite a bit of flint found locally and spent many hours this past winter chipping points for the arrows. Jeremy had become expert with a bow and could split a wild plum out of a tree that grew nearby.

Jeremy still had his dad's pistol and he had the rifle he found wrapped in oilskins with the wagon. He found ammunition for the rifle but had never fired it for the same reason he didn't shoot his father's pistol near his cave house. The sound might attract someone to investigate. However, he kept the rifle and pistol clean and in working order. He explained to Timmy about the guns,

"This pistol is primed and ready to fire but there's no need for you to touch it or mess with it. When you're old enough, I'll teach you about it and the rifle." He continued,

"I want you to be good with the bow and arrow. They're silent. You can be a lot quieter with a bow than you can with a rifle."

The training went on throughout the fall and winter. Soon Timmy was hitting the mark chosen by Jeremy Deaver. Timmy could shoot a rabbit at ten or more paces and he killed his first deer with a fifteen-yard shot from his bow. The boy was sad and proud at the same time. Jeremy convinced the boy that what he had done was what humans had been doing since the first man. If you were to survive, you had to take a life.

Out on the prairie, Adam Sanders rode right up to Bob Dove and offered his hand. Bob shook the hand.

Sanders said, "Bob? What are ya doing here on + I range?"

Bob Dove looked at Sanders without a smile and said, Sanders? They ain't neither one of us on + I range here... We're more west of + I.. We're all on open range and we all probably lookin for the same thing."

Sanders laughed a small unconvincing laugh and said, "Well .... Bob. You might be right at that. On both counts."

Tom Hale asked, Bob? How many of them calves you found by now?"

Bob Dove said, "Adam. Why don't you boys go back your direction and me and my partner will go back our direction before something goes wrong out here?"

Adam Sanders said, "Who is your partner? Ain't ya gonna interduce us?"

Bob Dove said, "This here's B. B. Kelly. Kelly that's Adam Sanders, Tom Hale, Shorty Meeks and I don't know that other fellah."

Sanders said, "That's Frank Jolly. He come around after you pulled stakes to go see about your sister."

Adam Sanders said, "Bob? I don't know if you know, but old Charlie died and now Granger is runnin the + I."

Bob Dove winced and said, "Damn. I liked ole Charlie... Granger's too full of hisself. He's gonna be hard to work for I bet."

Adam said, "Well ... It don't matter but just so you know, I'm Segundo and I ride for the + I *all the way*! Whatever Granger says, is the way it'll be. It won't be healthy for you and your partner to be caught on + I range. Period."

The two groups parted company and each went a different direction. Bob Dove felt like he'd been threatened with his death if he was caught on the + I. He told B. B. Kelly,

"I hope we find ever damned cow with the E 4 and they don't find any!!"

Bob and B. B. rode west, southwest looking for cattle. There was a slight chill in the air, but it was a welcome change from the heat they had been experiencing those last few weeks of summer. They came across some cattle but no E 4 cows and no unbranded calves. After riding five miles or more, they turned back north. There was so much country to see and two men could only see so much. They took advantage of every high spot they could in hopes of seeing a bigger scope of the land.

Finally, they spotted small dots in the far distance. Bob Dove pointed them out and said, "Looky there... Ya see 'em?"

B. B. Kelly looked and said, "Ya sure them ain't buffler?"

Bob Dove said, "They ain't ... Buffalo stay packed tighter together. Them's cows. Now we gotta go see, who's cows, is they?"

It took an hour to cross low spots, dodge brush and mesquites, wind through arroyos until they finally got the cattle in sight again. There was a good-sized herd here scattered with various brands. Dove noticed a few unbranded calves, but they appeared too young to be weaned off their mothers. The E 4 brand didn't show up right off but eventually, they would see some. When they spotted the E 4 cows, they checked to see if the cow still had a calf following her. They kept combing through the big scattered herd and moving the ones they wanted northeast, back toward the Ewing holdings.

In the mix, any unbranded calves that they saw would be watched to see if a mama was nearby. They came to a low spot with plenty of grass and a small water hole.

Dove said, "Let's try to hold these cattle here and let 'em set for a while."

Kelly said, "Good idea, I'll gather up some wood and make a fire."

Bob rode through the cattle, checking brands and especially taking a close look at any unbranded calves. When he found a brand other than the E 4, he worked them back toward the cattle they'd combed through. B. B. Kelly was stretched out by the small fire watching and admiring the patience of his partner. He grinned to himself. Bob Dove fancied himself a doer of bad deeds. An *outlaw*.

Kelly said to himself aloud, "Bob Dove, you ain't no outlaw."

The final gather of E 4 cattle was fifty-eight cows and sixty-six unbranded calves. Dove and Kelly kept driving them north and taking turns looking for more cattle roaming the countryside. They had pushed these cattle nearly twenty miles from where they were found. The cattle were content to move along slowly, grazing the lush grass at their own chosen speed as they went. When a water hole could be found, The men would hold them close by and make a camp for the night. The men knew they should be getting close to the Ewing range by now.

Captain Lowe was leading six rangers with him on the way back from Abilene. The rangers came upon a small water hole. They were letting their horses drink and the men dismounted for a small reprieve from their saddles. There were fresh horse tracks mixed with cattle tracks.

The Captain said, "Somebody, follow them tracks and see if whoever it is wants to sell some beef to us for the station."

The murmur of low voices could be heard but no one volunteered. Captain Lowe wasn't really a patient man, but he waited to see if anyone was going to speak up. After ten minutes went by Lowe said,

"Buckley! You and Fisk. Catch your horses and start following those tracks. If you don't find anyone in three hours, head northeast and catch up with us on the Slayton Springs trail."

The two Texas rangers, Buckley and Fisk followed the tracks several miles before deciding they were more than a day behind the cattle and those who were driving them. They cut west and eventually found the Slayton Springs trail. In it were the tracks of their fellow rangers and Captain Lowe. The clouds were promising a rare Texas snowstorm.

Jeremy Deaver kept up his training of Timmy, teaching him which plants were safe and which ones to stay away from. He taught him various ways to build a quick shelter in almost every kind of terrain. He taught the boy how to strip the deer meat and hang it to cure. Timmy was a bright and willing student and picked things up quickly. He was reading aloud from the Bible and with the exception of a few bigger words, he was reading to Jeremy's satisfaction.

Winter set in with a small skiff of snow that lasted only overnight. By mid-day the following day, the only evidence that there had been snow was under trees and in the brush where the sun's rays didn't reach. Another week of mild weather and then the cold wind came out of the north. It started getting colder by the hour and by nighttime, the snow was falling in waves and piling up on the north side of any vegetation it could cling to. The drifts were getting higher each time Jeremy went outside to get more wood to feed the hungry fire.

The following morning, Deaver had to put his weight against the door to get it open. Timmy and Chapo peaked out the door and then stepped outside to relieve themselves. It was as cold as Jeremy ever remembered it being. He had seen this much snow only once in his life before. The man and boy spent twenty minutes hauling and stacking firewood inside the cabin. Jeremy went to the small stream, but it was frozen over in the spot where he liked to fill the water bucket. Instead, he scooped up a bucketful of pure snow and took it in to set close to the hearth.

Timmy asked, "What we gonna do today, dad?"

Jeremy said, "We'll stay in. We can sleep, you can read to us from the Good Book. We can't do anything out there. We have food and water. We have wood for the fire. Tomorrow might be different."

Timothy asked, "Dad? Are we gonna get some horses? Someday?"

Jeremy answered, "We might someday but I'm glad we don't have any to worry about today."

That seemed to satisfy Timmy. Soon, he and Chapo were curled up in the corner sound asleep. Jeremy pulled out some of the soft buckskin he'd been working with and started making a winter shirt for Timmy. That night, the wind died down and the next day the sun came out. Timmy and Chapo played in the snow as the day warmed up. Soon, Timmy's clothes were soaking wet from the snow. Jeremy had Timmy go inside the cabin, strip down and hang his clothes close to the hearth to dry.

A man rode into the meadow as Jeremy was cutting more wood to stack. Jeremy knew that Timmy and Chapo were inside.

Deaver looked up from his chore and said, "Hello Mister. Something I can do for you?"

The man sat his horse and studied all the marked-up snow where the boy and dog had been playing. The man could think of no reason for the marks. He said, "I could use some water if ya got some."

Jeremy grabbed the cup he kept handy for getting water out of the stream. He then went to the edge of the water where the melting of the ice permitted the water to flow and filled the cup. He took it to the man, saying,

"Here ya are." He handed the cup to the man and said,

"What ya doin' in these parts?"

The man drank the water, handed the cup back to Jeremy and said,

"Thanks. I'm just huntin cattle. I ride for the + I outfit."

Deaver said, "Pleased to oblige."

Frank Jolly said, "I'm prowlin the country, lookin for cattle. I'll head back, see if I can meet up with my Boss, Granger Ingraham and a couple other riders with us. We'll camp on the Salt Fork of the Brazos around dark. Thanks for the water, I 'ppreciate it."

Names had not been given at this time. Frank Jolly rode east, southeast as he left the meadow. Deaver watched him for quite a while as the man was in no hurry. He rode across the meadow, ever watchful for tracks or sign. Finally, the man disappeared into the trees on the ridge.

Timmy came out with his half-dried clothes on. Jeremy reprimanded him and sent him back inside to finish drying his clothes. Supper was just coffee, fried deer meat and water gravy that Jeremy made in his cast iron skillet.

Frank Jolly found the campfire where Granger Ingraham and the others were getting their supper together. Granger quizzed Frank about anything and everything he might have seen. Jolly said that he saw no cow tracks made since the snow and told about coming into the meadow and finding a squatter there.

Granger Ingraham asked, "What's a fellah doin' there?"

Frank Jolly said, "He's got a cabin built back into a small hill. He was cutting wood when I rode in. Somethin had disturbed a lot of the snow around him but I can't figure out what. I just know it sure wasn't cattle. I didn't see nobody else around and there wasn't a horse track or cow track made anywhere since the snow. He ain't a rancher and there ain't no sign of him farmin."

One of the other men asked, "Who's range are we on Boss?"

Granger answered, "Might be Ewing's. We're too far north and west to be on the + I."

Frank Jolly asked, "We on Ewing range lookin for E 4 cattle?"

Granger Ingraham didn't answer right away, and he didn't like what Jolly's question implied. He looked at Frank Jolly and said,

"If you don't like your job, you can ride … Any direction you want."

Ingraham stood up and walked to the edge of the circle of men around the fire to relieve himself. Frank Jolly sat thinking about the challenge he was just given. In other words, Granger is saying, *'I'm going onto another man's range, a dead man's range and driving his cattle to my range so that I can brand his calves in*

payment for the dead man's cattle being on my range?'
In Frank Jolly's view, that was stealing.

Chapter 15

Bob Dove and B. B. Kelly had eventually picked up close to two hundred head of E 4 cows and about that many unbranded calves with them. They followed the cattle, herding them in the direction of the Ewing holdings. They struggled through an unusual snowstorm and finally got the cattle close to the corrals. The corrals were too small to hold all the cattle, so the two men worked very slow and cautiously as they put the calves in the corral. There were only a few cows bawling for their own calf although cattle are going to bawl just because others are doing it. Three days later, B. B. Kelly counted two hundred eighteen unbranded calves in the corral.

Bob Dove said, "We got a nice start on a place of our own here. We get these calves branded with the B reverse B; we'll have a pocket full of money."

"We still *squattin* on this place. Too bad we can't find a place to start our own outfit."

Then a thought came to Kelly. He asked, "How we gonna brand this many calves by ourselves. We could workday and night and it still take a week."

Bob Dove answered, "We just gotta do it. You and me. Ain't nobody else."

Dove swung his arms and turned to look around and was saying, "You see anybody else?" His voice faded.

Just as he turned, a man was riding into the yard.

"Hello." The man hollered, trying to be heard over the noise the cattle were making.

Bob Dove looked at B. B. Kelly and said, "I'll do the talkin."

Frank Jolly waited to be invited to step down from his horse. He introduced himself and mentioned that he had been with Adam Sanders on the day that they accidently met up on the prairie more than a month earlier. Bob Dove recognized the man.

After the introductions were made, Dove asked Jolly what his plans were. Jolly answered,

"I'm out of a job right now. Just left Granger Ingraham's + I outfit night before last. I got a little grub and water, my bedroll, my rifle and these clothes. That's it."

B. B. Kelly wanted to speak but Bob Dove had told him to be quiet. Bob looked at Kelly, turned to Frank Jolly and said:

"We could use a hand for a day or two. Got these calves to brand. We can feed ya and pay ya a little. Ya interested?"

Frank Jolly said, "I can stick around for a day or two. I ain't in no hurry except it's winter and they shore ain't no job a huntin' me."

Bob Dove told him. "Find a place if ya can. We just fixin to start cleaning this snow off for a place to brand these calves."

The three men worked with shovels and a flat board to clear the snow in one corner of the corral where the calves could be worked. They all knew that a wet hide doesn't brand very well.

Two men with ropes, heading and heeling the calves and one man on the ground putting the hot iron on the hides of the calves and cutting the testicles out of the bull calves, rendering them incapable of reproducing. The work was getting done very smoothly. The men switched positions as needed to rest horses. Dove and Kelly were impressed with Frank Jolly. The man sure could rope. Nobody was ever waiting for him to catch either the head or the hind feet of the calves.

After the first day, a rough count showed the three men had worked well over one hundred head of calves. The fresh branded heifer calves were turned out with the cows. The fire was started for the supper to be prepared. The shack the two men had thrown together was small and not well built, but by the time it was getting dark, all three men had their bed rolls spread out on the dirt floor. At least they had a roof over their heads and weren't having to sleep in the snow.

The grub supply was low and with three men eating, they needed supplies. Frank Jolly had suggested keeping the steer calves in the corral overnight to keep an eye on them and Bob Dove was as jealous as he was thankful for the suggestion.

If a fresh castrated steer calf went off and died somewhere out in the surrounding area, no one would know till the buzzards showed up. If one died in the corral, the meat could be salvaged. Cowboys didn't get to eat a lot of beef unless a cow or calf broke a leg or had some other misfortunate accident. They relied on wild game. Anything from a rabbit to a buffalo. Sure enough, the next morning, a freshly cut steer had bled to death which was the case sometimes after being cut.

Frank Jolly helped the two men finish branding the rest of the calves and mounted up. He had said his goodbyes and left with a good-sized chunk of meat from the dead calf wrapped up in the slicker tied behind his saddle. As he rode away Kelly said,

"That fellah sure showed up at the right time, and he's a good hand too."

Bob Dove seemed irritated at the comment and said,

"Aww ... He wuddn't nothin special."

The freshly branded calves were finally turned out and a plan was made. If the weather looked like it was going to be agreeable, the men would wait a couple weeks and pick up ten to fifteen head and drive them to Fort Belknap to sell and get resupplied.

Jeremy Deaver was once again, cutting wood when something caught his eye. Movement in the trees on the ridge above the meadow. He said, fairly loud, but without shouting,

"Timmy! Chapo. Go Hide!"

There was still quite a bit of snow on the ground, but much had melted and turned into mud as well. Timmy and Chapo weren't far from the cabin and had to make a decision whether to go inside or hide in the trees behind the cabin. Timmy didn't know why Jeremy had said to hide but he already knew if Jeremy said to do it, that's all he needed to know for now. It was coming on towards evening and once the sun went down, the temperature was going to drop pretty fast. Timmy decided to go inside the cabin. Chapo followed him.

Jeremy watched from the corner of his eye as the boy and the dog went inside and closed the door. Jeremy wasn't going to have time to explain. He would have to trust Timmy to stay hidden until it was safe.

Frank Jolly rode through the last of the trees and into the open ground of the meadow. He called to Jeremy, "Hello the house!"

Jeremy straightened up from his work and stretched as he put his left hand on the small of his back. He responded, "Hello... Come on in."

Frank Jolly was riding a different horse and Jeremy made a mental note of that fact. The same man had been here several days earlier. That could mean the man lived fairly close by.

Frank Jolly pulled his horse to a stop and said, "Old timer, You're still doin what you was doin the other day."

Jeremy was wiping the sweat from his neck with his kerchief and said, "This wood heats ya up more than one time, and I guess I've got a hungry fire."

The man sat his mount waiting to be invited down. He chuckled and said,

"Guess I hadn't thought of that. but you're right."

Jeremy asked,

"Can I get ya some water? I got a cup inside the cabin. I'll go get it."

Deaver still hadn't invited the man to dismount. A man with range manners knew to stay mounted until asked to dismount. Frank Jolly said,

"Some water would be nice. Thanks."

Jeremy went inside long enough to grab the cup, but he said quietly,

"Stay put Timmy. I don't know how long he's gonna stick around."

Deaver came out of the cabin with the cup and walked the fifty feet to the stream. He said as he scooped fresh water into the cup,

"This water's hard to beat."

Jeremy walked up to the man sitting on his horse and handed the cup of water up to him. Jeremy said,

"My name's Jeremy. Jeremy Deaver. What's yours?

Jolly took the water and drank half a cup before answering. He said,

"That IS good water! Uh, my name is Frank. Frank Jolly."

Deaver said, "I recognized you as the fellah come by here a few days ago. You can get down if you like. Ya say you don't live around here?"

Frank Jolly dismounted, finished the water in the cup and walked to the stream for more. He said,

"Naw. I had been workin for Ingraham's, ya know. The Cross Eye? But, ever since ole Charlie died and the boy took over, I haven't been happy with some of the treatment. I met up with the boy, Granger, and we had words. My own horse, here, was with the remuda so I swapped horses and I rode out. I come upon two punchers over at the burned-out Ewing place and they needed some help putting a brand on the slicks. Maybe it wasn't right. But I guess somebody was gonna get them calves. Anyway, I helped 'em and they give me ten dollars and fed me while I was there."

Jeremy heard every word plain. The burned-out Ewing place. This was going to be an interesting conversation. Deaver figured listening to this man was going to be very informative. He said,

"Ya know it's gonna get dark before too long. Let me kick up this fire and fry some deer meat out here. My cabin's small and I wasn't expectin any company. You're welcome to spread your bedroll here on the ground. I got a buffler hide I'll bring out for ya."

Jeremy went back into the cabin. He quietly outlined his plan to Timmy. Jeremy took the rolled-up buffalo hide and spread it on the packed area under the brush arbor near the fire. Frank Jolly had already added sticks to the embers in the fire pit and was gathering up more wood. Jeremy noticed that Jolly had hobbled his horse several yards away.

Frank Jolly wasn't offended that the man didn't invite him into the cabin. Frank knew that this would be warmer than just about any other offer he could expect out here. If Frank would have rode on, he would have had to find a suitable place to spend the night and it wouldn't be better than this. Deaver came back from the cabin with some salt pork and the skillet. Frank noticed that everything appeared clean. Jeremy put the skillet on the fire and the coffee on to boil. He said, I'll go cut some meat and went back inside. Once he got in, he said quietly,

"Timmy, you and Chapo just sit tight. He'll ride out tomorrow. I'm sorry it's gotta be this way."

Frank enjoyed the deer meat and water gravy. Jeremy ate a small amount and said,

"I had some earlier. I'll save some of this for in the mornin."

Frank Jolly offered to help clean up the skillet, but Jeremy wouldn't hear of it. He said,

"Naw sir... I don't get a lot of company. You sit tight and I'll come back and we can swap a few lies."

Jeremy went into the cabin with the left-over fried deer meat and the gravy left in the skillet, which he gave to Timmy and Chapo for their supper. Jeremy then went back out to sit with his guest.

When Jeremy finally called it a night, he told Frank which way to ride toward Chinook Springs station and said good night to him. Frank answered back and crawled into his bedroll with the buffalo hide under it for insulation from the cold ground. The next morning, just at daylight, Jeremy opened his door to see the man and his horse gone. The buffalo hide had been carefully rolled up. Deaver looked around carefully before he allowed Timmy and Chapo outside to do their business.

Bob Dove and B. B. Kelly were driving an even dozen steers to Fort Belknap and were halfway there when they encountered Adam Sanders and three other riders. They knew they were, possibly on the southern edge of Ingraham's range. There was no use to run and there was no use to deny their location. They pulled their rifles but didn't aim them or threaten with them.

Adam Sanders rode up to Bob Dove and shook his head. He was chuckling a suppressed laugh. He said,

"Bob ... Damn it Bob!! You know you ain't supposed to be caught on the + I. ... Where the hell are you going with these calves?"

Bob said, "We's drivin 'em to Fort Belknap. We didn't find 'em here. We branded 'em two weeks ago. If you look, you can see these ain't real fresh brands."

All the while Bob was talking, Adam and Tom Hale were visually inspecting the calves. All of them wore the B reverse B and it was plain that the brands were a couple weeks old. Adam Sanders said,

"I can see what you're sayin… But, damnitt!! You two ain't on the Ingraham payroll and so, you're trespassing. Granger would want me to take these calves away from you. I see that they's all branded with… Is that ya'all's mark? The B reverse B?"

Sanders then said, "I'm takin three head fer ya usin Ingraham's + I range to get to Belknap. At least I ain't gunna kill ya, *this time*. Next time ya may not be so lucky."

Dove nodded. He and Kelly sat and watched Sanders' men cut three head out. He knew better than to say anything out loud.

Adams justified it by calling it a toll. Sanders wrote up a bill of sale for the three head on a piece of paper that one of the men had in his saddle bag and made Bob Dove sign it. Then he and his riders took the three calves and headed toward their home corrals.

Dove and Kelly took the remaining nine head on toward Fort Belknap. Bob Dove felt he'd been played for a fool and cussed the entire rest of the drive to Fort Belknap.

Chapter 16

Another year and a half had passed, and Timmy was growing fast. He was going on seven years old now, although Jeremy had no idea when the boy's birthday was. Jeremy and Timmy were into a rhythm with each other when it came to working. They teamed up on the buck saw and cut a lot of firewood and plenty of good, straight oaks from the timber nearby. Jeremy knew how to split the logs into fours and use the quarters for a fence. There had been occasional cattle wander into the lush, green meadow and Jeremy didn't want to let them make a mess around his cabin, arbor and firepit. Timmy's education continued as Jeremy still read from the Bible and required Timmy to sound out letters and also reproduce them in the dirt with a stick. Any scrap of paper that they might come in contact with, was seen as a chance to write on it with the charcoal tip of a burnt stick.

Twice, Jeremy made the trek to Chinook Springs Station with Timmy and Chapo along. Timmy and Chapo stayed hidden while Jeremy Deaver bought supplies. Jeremy made sure the Ewing boy had clothes. He modified them to fit the growing boy and he still made their buckskins from the hides of deer that they survived on. When Timmy grew out of a pair of pants from the trading post, Deaver would stitch a piece of buckskin in between the pants material on the outside of the leg and add some buckskin onto the bottoms. Deaver was keeping his hair shorter and his face shaved.

Occasionally, a rider would wander into the meadow and Jeremy would host them with a meal and coffee. Frank Jolly stopped by every chance he had. Bob Dove and B. B. Kelly would ride by if they were close also. Randle Sneed and Samuel Blair had stopped by recently and Jeremy Deaver felt like Sneed was getting a little too inquisitive and was always trying to pry an answer out of him. Timothy and Chapo would hide whenever anyone came around.

Timmy and Chapo were experts at hiding, either inside or outside the cabin and remaining out of sight. They stayed on the alert and Chapo sure did a fine job of knowing when a rider was approaching. The last time Sneed and Blair had visited, Jeremy picked up on the increase of questions to Deaver about his background. One evening at the fire pit under the arbor, Sneed asked,

"Deaver? You ever been over on the Yellow House?"

Of course, that was where Jeremy had lived in the cave for so many years undetected. However, Deaver didn't know what the name of the cliff was. He answered,

"I been a few places, but I don't recall a place by that name."

Randle Sneed fancied himself a judge of when a person was lying or telling the truth. He looked into Jeremy's eyes and asked,

"Did you used to live up north on the Palo Duro?"

Jeremy did not hesitate to answer,

"Yes ... That where my pap and mother raised me up. They died and there was nothin to hold me there."

Deaver was good at not telling everything if it could be avoided. By this time, he knew the war between the states was over and although there remained some hard feelings between the ones who fought for the south against the *"damn yankees"* and vice versa, the ones from the north who fought the *"Johnny Rebs."* There seemed no real repercussion against those who didn't fight at all. Only an occasional remark. Randle Sneed asked,

"Jeremy, did you join the rebs or the yanks? Not that it makes any difference to me.. I'm just curious."

Jeremy Deaver looked at the ranger and said truthfully,

"I was too old to join. And I didn't wanna fight nobody. I managed to stay out of it. I had this thought in my head about me bein behind a barricade of some kind and somebody shootin at me. Somebody I didn't want killin me and somebody I didn't want to have to kill. If that makes me a coward in your eyes, then I guess, to you I'm a coward. To me, I'm alive and don't want to take the life of anybody. Not for anything."

Sneed knew he had just heard the truth from this man. He said,

"Naw. That don't make you no coward in my eyes."

The subject changed when Blair said,

"I wonder what ever happened to that Ewing boy? He needs to be found or them squatters is gonna end up owning that nice ranch and all the unbranded calves from them Ewing mama cows."

Jeremy wanted to hear more about the legal aspect of this. He asked,

"What does all that mean?"

Sneed outlined the situation and it helped him form a basic understanding. If the Ewing boy was found and positively identified, he could still rightly claim the Ben Ewing holdings. If he didn't claim it soon, the two men known as Bob Dove and B. B. Kelly, who had rebuilt a shack to live in, for proof of residence, could claim the whole thing. Land and cattle.

Jeremy was careful to ask any follow up questions about the Ewing boy. He felt the suspicions from Sneed this visit and he thought Randle Sneed had been doing some investigating. He only wanted what was best for Timmy. He asked,

"If that boy is still alive, how'd anybody know him from any other boy his size?"

Samuel Blair was sitting there, mostly not saying much but felt like taking part in the conversation. Blair answered,

"Timothy Ewing has got a noticeable birthmark on the left side of his face. He was just four years old when the Injuns kilt his family and burnt the place down. The boy disappeared and it was first thought that the Injuns took him. We been watchin them Injuns real close and we have seen no signs that he was ever with them. We even done some tradin and got some white kids back from another tribe that traded horses for them white kids and he wadn't with 'em."

Sneed interjected,

"The boy's body hasn't been found but we are pretty certain that the boy made it to the Yellow House and somebody, we don't know if a white man or some kind of Injun, was takin care of him. We found a rock wall in front of a cave where they lived for some time. When we got close to the place, they disappeared. We tried trackin 'em but *that somebody* sure knows how to hide a trail."

Blair picked up the conversation again,

"Like I say, this boy has a mark on his face. The neighbor that described the boy says it's big enough to catch most of the left side of his face. Says it's a reddish-purple color."

Randle Sneed looked right at Jeremy Deaver and said,

"I Think ..." He paused just for a couple seconds and began again,

"I mean, I believe you have seen this boy. You may even know where he is or what has happened to him. If I'm right, You're that same wild lookin character we seen on the flats in that ole abandon shack a couple years ago. It can't hurt you or the boy as far as any laws bein broke, but It would be a good thing for you to do to let him claim what's rightfully his."

Jeremy felt the tears forming in his eyes and there was no stopping them. His heart was hurting at the very thought of having to give Timmy up to these men. He felt that they were good men from the first time he spied on them at their campfire on the Yellow House rim and every time he saw them since then. Jeremy asked,

"How can he claim his ranch and who would take care of him?"

Sneed said,

"If you can find him or if you know where he is, bring him to the Slayton Springs Ranger station to Captain Marcus Lowe. Now, Captain Lowe is a fair man and he'll listen to you. If he can determine that he's the boy named Timothy Ewing, who would be around seven years old now, is the survivor of the Indian massacre, Capitan Lowe will go through the proper channels to get the boy placed in the company of a responsible adult and see to it that the boy claims what is rightfully his."

All these big words were floating over the head of a man with a terrible heartache at the thought of giving Timmy up to the authorities and maybe never seeing him again. He would give his own life to save the boy, but should he lose him, he might as well not keep on living.

Apparently, Sneed read the mind of Jeremy Deaver and could see that his suspicions were on target. This man was the cave dweller and the shaggy mountain man from the abandon shack on those wind-swept flats.

He was sure, this man knew where the Ewing boy was. Sneed also knew he would have to handle things softly from this point on. Sneed asked Blair to tend to their horses so he could talk privately with Deaver. After Blair was a distance off, tending to the horses, Randle Sneed said,

"Jeremy? ... Do you have that boy hid out somewhere?"

Deaver broke down and wept openly. He looked at ranger Sneed and couldn't stop the tears. He pointed to the cabin but couldn't say anything. Sneed was a smart man and gave Jeremy time to try to pull himself together. He wanted to go into the cabin but thought it would be better if Jeremy could get the boy to come out. Randle Sneed felt much sorrow for this man. He was sure the man was attached to the boy and didn't want to give him up. Sneed felt his own eyes starting to tear up. Deaver recovered a little composure and stood up. He let out a big sigh and walked toward the cabin and opened the door. He called inside,

"Timmy? Come with me. These rangers want to help you."

Randle Sneed watched as the boy and his faithful dog emerged from the cabin door. Sneed stood up and the dog got in front of Timmy's legs, shielding him from a possible threat. Jeremy turned to Sneed and motioned him to sit back down on the stump by the firepit. As soon as Sneed sat back down, the dog came forward cautiously while Deaver was telling Chapo,

"It's alright Chapo. Easy…"

Chapo went into his low growl and the hair on his back stood up like bristles on a brush. Jeremy said to Sneed,

"Let the dog come to you. Don't try to touch him and don't make any sudden moves."

Then Deaver said to Chapo,

"Chapo. Easy. It's alright. See?"

Deaver walked to Sneed and stood by him. Chapo crept ever so slowly toward the seated man and once he got within five feet, he sniffed the man. He then, relaxed, and went to the man as if to say, *'I accept this man to have a good heart'*.

Sneed could see the boy was in good physical shape and well cared for. It was evident that Deaver had taken good care of him. Sneed could also, plainly see the splotch birthmark on the boy's left cheek. Timothy Ewing was alive and well.

Randle Sneed asked Deaver if he would accompany the rangers and the boy back to Slayton Springs in the morning. Deaver had gotten his composure back enough to nod his head in agreement. Timothy was sitting as close to Jeremy as he could get and Chapo was right in front of both of them.

Chapter 17

Captain Marcus Lowe watched as the group approached the ranger office. He recognized Randle Sneed who had a rider behind him. Sam Blair was riding with someone riding behind him as well and there was a dog following. He shaded his eyes trying to make sense of the odd spectacle. Sneed stopped his mount and a youngster slid off from behind Sneed's saddle. Another person, a grown man, slid from the back of Blair's saddle then Blair dismounted. Sneed dismounted and walked up the few steps to Captain Lowe and said,

"Captain?" His voice cracked with emotion as he said, "We've got the Ewing boy."

Sneed also immediately said, "Captain? Keep your hands off the boy until the dog accepts you. And, Captain… I'm *serious*."

Captain Lowe stood like a statue as the dog came up the stairs and sniffed the captain. As soon as the dog relaxed, Sneed turned to Timmy and said,

"Timmy? This is Captain Lowe. He's a good man. You know that because Chapo likes him."

Sneed turned to Jeremy Deaver and said,

"Jeremy Deaver? This is Captain Marcus Lowe. Uh, Captain? This man is Jeremy Deaver and he has saved the boy's life and taken good care of him all this time. I could tell you more, but I'll write it in my report. For now, all I want to say is, the man and the boy and the dog need NOT be separated. They need to stay together."

Captain Lowe had Deaver and Timothy come inside his office. He shut the door before Chapo could come inside and Chapo started barking and growling as he scratched incessantly on the door to the Captain's office. Sneed opened the door and let Chapo in. As soon as the dog was inside, he became quiet and curled up at Timmy's feet. The Captain asked Deaver some questions and he spoke to Timothy as well. He was seated at his desk and then thought to offer some coffee to Jeremy Deaver. As he stood up and started around the desk, Chapo became bristled and standing between Timmy and the Captain. The Captain said,

"I just want to get some coffee for Mr. Deaver."

Chapo kept his body between the Captain and Timmy, maneuvering around as he allowed the Captain to reach the stove and pour a cup of coffee to hand to Deaver. He said,

"Well... I can see Timothy has had a good bodyguard on his adventure."

Jeremy told Captain Lowe,

"The boy's feet were bloody, raw and full of cactus thorns. He could hardly walk. I was livin in that cave for a lot of years and didn't want nothin to do with people. This boy and his dog come to me and I knowed I'd have to take care of him. I dodged everybody, red men and white men for years. All I had was my Bible and whatever food I needed. I skinned animals and made what I had to have. I feel like God above give me this boy and I guess he give me to the boy too. The boy needed me. I guess I needed the boy too but I didn't know it."

Captain Lowe sat pondering the situation. Him being the Captain of the Texas Rangers in this region made him the top law officer around here but just how much authority did he have over this case? He didn't know.

Captain Lowe wanted to talk to Timothy alone and he asked Deaver to step outside for a few minutes. He asked Jeremy to take Chapo with him. Jeremy said plainly,

"He won't go. Not without Timmy."

Captain Lowe decided the dog could stay.

He asked Timmy, "Boy? Do you know what your name is?"

Timmy said, "Timmy."

Captain Lowe asked, "Is it Timothy? Timothy Ewing?"

Timmy looked puzzled and answered, "Mama called me Timothy. Dad calls me Timmy."

Captain Lowe looked perplexed. He said, Your father is alive? I thought your whole family had been ... "

He caught himself. He then said, "Where is your dad?"

Timmy pointed out the door and said, "There. Outside."

Captain Lowe sprung to his feet and Chapo stood and growled loudly as he openly displayed that he would protect the boy. The Captain looked out the window nearest him and all he could see was Jeremy Deaver standing talking to Randle Sneed. He then had a thought.

He asked, "Do you call Jeremy, "Dad?"

Timmy pointed to the closed door and said again, "Dad."

Captain Lowe asked Timmy, "Do you know where your Father's ... I mean, Do you know where the Ben Ewing place is?"

Timmy shook his head 'no'.

Finally, Captain Lowe let Sneed take Timmy, Chapo and Jeremy to the cook shack to get them fed and then to an empty bunking area. They would be guests of the Texas Rangers until Captain Lowe could figure the way to proceed.

Jeremy wanted to have this over with. He just wanted to get back to the little cabin where he and Timmy and Chapo were at home. He dearly loved that place. If there was any drawbacks to it, it would have to be that quite a lot of folks now knew where it was and liked to stop by. If this kept up, there would be a heavily traveled path and then it may become a road. Jeremy liked his solitude. At least now, he wouldn't have to hide Timmy when someone came around. After two days at the ranger station, Captain Lowe and Randle Sneed set out to accompany Jeremy Deaver, Timmy and Chapo back to the cabin in the meadow.

Captain Lowe had learned enough to know that the boy loved Deaver and Deaver loved the boy. He saw no reason to disrupt the relationship. He was convinced that Jeremy hid the boy for so long as his way of protecting him. Jeremy had confessed that he hid in the brush and listened to Sneed and Blair as they discussed Timothy Ewing. Deaver started calling the boy, 'Timmy'. The boy didn't know what his last name was at first but now, it rolled off his tongue easily.

The rangers outfitted Jeremy and Timmy with a horse each along with saddles and everything they needed. They replenished their food supplies as well. Randle Sneed went through the cook shack and found an enamel coffee pot, some enamel plates and cups as well. He knew Deaver could use them at his cabin.

They arrived at the cabin and noticed no disturbance. Captain Lowe and Randle Sneed spent the night and left out the next day at daylight saying, they would be in touch as to the next step in Timothy Ewing claiming his rightful ownership of the Ewing holdings. That included all the E 4 cattle and any monies that could be recovered. Jeremy was somewhat relieved that Timmy wasn't taken away from him, but he was at least a little worried about what might transpire later.

Ranger Sneed drew a rough map as they rode along and for future reference, calculated the area where Jeremy had built his cabin. He knew there was a large map in San Antonio and he also knew that he would be going there within the next month. This is where he could establish the scope of the Ben Ewing holdings.

Chapter 18

Bob Dove and B. B. Kelly stayed busy gathering as many E 4 cattle as they could find. They had returned several times and sold calves to Fort Belknap for beef. They hadn't improved the dwelling on the Ewing place, but they had built some decent, useable, working corrals. They never knew when, on the range looking for E 4 cattle, they might run across some of the Ingraham crew out doing the same thing, Looking for E 4 cattle. They were more cautious to avoid Ingraham range because the tariff was too high. Granger had even made several threats to kill anybody caught on his range.

Bob Dove was calculating the amount of cattle they had gathered against what he believed Ewing owned. They were probably more than half. The two men, riding miles and miles for many weeks had managed to gather nearly five hundred head. Some of the cows had calves and some did not. It's easy to tell a cow that has raised a calf and one that did not. When a cow is raising a calf, they don't gain weight like a cow that doesn't have to make milk to sustain a calf. The number of calves Bob Dove and B. B. Kelly had branded was not much over four hundred. Still, the two felt wealthy knowing that many calves wore their B reverse B brand.

Frank Jolly rode into the meadow one late afternoon with a small deer carcass on his horse. He hollered the customary greeting,

"Hello the camp!"

Jeremy Deaver came out of the willows by the stream with a small stringer of fish. Right behind him came a boy and a dog. This took Frank Jolly by surprise. He sat his horse outside the split rail fence near the arbor.

As soon as Jeremy recognized him, he said, "Get down Frank. Set here and we'll fix you some catfish."

Frank Jolly said, "I got a little deer about a mile from here. It's good and fresh. I'll give ya most of it, but right now, catfish sounds good."

The two men shook hands and Jeremy introduced Frank to Timmy. Chapo was standoffish for a few minutes but he finally accepted Jolly. Jeremy explained about Timmy and told the important parts of the story. When Frank heard that this was the Ewing boy, he let out a whistle and shook his head. Jeremy hesitated with what he was saying and looked at Frank. He asked,

"What? ... You heard of this boy?"

Frank said, "Oh yeah! I sure did. I know a lot of folks been looking for him. There for a while, right after it happened, folks were scourin the countryside for him. Then a lot of folks thought the Comanche took him. How'd you come to have him?"

"That dog there, protected the boy. You can't get near the boy if Chapo don't want you to. The dog led him to me in that cave. I seen 'em comin off that other side and I knowed something was wrong with the boy. He wadn't just right when Chapo brung him to me. I figger that dog knew I could help the boy. We been together ever since."

They ate catfish and talked quite a while and finally Frank Jolly said,

"I know where his pap's place is. The burned-out ranch. It ain't all that far."

Jeremy said, "Captain Lowe of the Texas Rangers is goin into it. Findin out what comes next for the boy to claim his ranch. He's s'pose to check in San Antone and come back here with what takes place next."

Frank Jolly said, "The burned-out house is east and a little north from here. I been to it. They's two fellers squattin on it. Feller named Bob Dove and …"

Before Jolly could finish his sentence, Jeremy said,

"B. B. Kelly…?"

Frank asked, "You know them boys?"

Deaver answered, "They come here ever once in a while. They ain't never seen the boy. They don't know he's here."

Frank Jolly said, "They're gatherin all the E 4 cattle, strippin the calves off and brandin 'em B reverse B."

Jolly drew the brand in the dirt with a stick.

Frank continued, "I don't know it's wise to let either one them see the boy or let them find out he's alive and livin here."

Jeremy looked puzzled. Jolly said, "If something happens to Timmy before this ranger Captain places the boy on his own place, them squatters are most likely gonna get the ranch and all it's holdings ... If somebody don't rightfully claim it in the eyes of the law."

Jeremy thought of the two men. He didn't want to believe that they would do anything bad to Timmy. He sure didn't want to take any chances with Timmy's life.

He said, "What am I gonna do? How can I protect him?"

Then he said, "I guess, he better hide like before when somebody comes around."

Frank said, "Look. I ain't gotta be anywhere. I quit my job up north and I'm just driftin. If you want, I'll stay here and help you keep an eye on the boy. Four eyes are better than two."

Deaver thought about it. Frank Jolly didn't appear to be the kind of man that would hurt anybody. Still, the man couldn't be expected to hang around here not making any money. Jeremy said,

"When Timmy takes his ranch back. I mean, when he *gets* his ranch back, he's gonna need somebody to help run things that knows about cattle. If you can stay around till then, You could come to work for Timmy. You could be in charge of the cow operation."

Frank Jolly said, "That sounds like a good deal to me." Then he said,

"I won't need much money for now. I still got some pay from the last job. Just food and a place to lay down at night."

Jolly pointed at the young deer hangin nearby that he'd brought in a few hours earlier and said,

"I can help with the larder around here."

They sat near the fire and talked for a couple hours after Timmy and Chapo went to the cabin. Jeremy had brought the buffalo robe to Frank and Frank spread it out on the ground. This would be *home* for a while.

Ranger Capitan Marcus Lowe and Ranger Randle Sneed came back from San Antonio with a detailed map of that particular part of Texas. Much of the area was uncharted except for the major water ways and a few other landmarks. The map clearly showed the area belonging to the Ben Ewing estate. They were also able to find a bank account for Ben Ewing's E 4 Cattle Company. The money in the bank couldn't be released to anyone but Timothy Ewing and he would have to be there in person. Captain Lowe sent Randle Sneed, Samuel Blair and John Fisk to locate the Ben Ewing headquarters and secure it for the rightful owner, Timothy Ewing. Captain Lowe and Harry Buckley rode out to find Jeremy Deaver and Timothy Ewing.

Chapter 19

Bob Dove and B. B. Kelly were out looking for more E 4 cattle when Randle Sneed and his two companions found the burned-out ranch house and barn of Ben Ewing. They saw the crude shack someone had thrown together a little more than a year earlier. They noticed ten or fifteen unbranded calves in the corral. Two of the calves were bawling with their mothers on the outside of the corral bawling as well. The cows were branded E 4. Sneed opened the gate and let all the calves out.

With no one around, the rangers looked in the crude shack and found a few personal items belonging to whoever put up the shack. There were a couple dirty bedrolls lying on the dirt floor and some dirty shirts and pants piled up on the floor in one corner. There was a pair of torn, red long handle underwear hanging on a nail. Blair picked up a branding iron with a B on one end and showed it to Sneed. The shack wouldn't keep a cold wind out or any heat in. Sneed wanted to tear it down, but he figured there would be time. He wanted to wait until the occupants showed up.

Randle Sneed knew quite a lot about cattle so he and the other two rode through any cattle they spotted and were checking for brands. There was a good amount of calves wearing fresh brands. All Branded with the B reverse B. Someone had been gathering the Ewing cattle. It didn't take a genius to figure it out. He explained it to Fisk and Blair,

"They squat here and they keep the E 4 cattle close by, but they brand the unbranded, weaned off calves with their brand. This: *B reverse B* we keep seein. They have nobody to say they can't claim the calves because the calves ain't gonna pair up with their mothers once they's weaned. They don't bother with the brands on the mothers because they don't need to. As long as the mothers keep raisin babies, they keep getting the calf crop. The heifers they put their B reverse B on, grow up and have calves. Them and those calves become the property of the owners of the B reverse B." He paused and said,

"It's a good thing we know that Timothy Ewing is alive and will take possession of his pap's ranch and the cattle and everything that goes with it."

Capitan Marcus Lowe and Harry Buckley had left out of Slayton Springs before the sun was up. They easily found the meadow and rode in. Lowe yelled,

"Hello the cabin!"

Just then, they heard the crack of a rifle. It came from behind the cabin. Capitan Lowe and Harry Buckley drew their side arms, not knowing what to expect. They heard another shot and someone yell excitedly, *'Ya got it!'* Capitan Lowe fired his pistol into the ground and said, again,

"Hello the Cabin!"

Jeremy Deaver came out of the trees behind the cabin carrying his homemade bow and a quiver full of arrows with Timmy carrying a rifle and Chapo with them.

There was another man as well and he, also was carrying a rifle. Jeremy waved and hollered,

"Captain Lowe. Get down and have some coffee. I'll fry you some meat and taters."

The introductions were made and they all sat around the fire pit under the arbor. Deaver explained that Frank and Jeremy were giving Timmy a lesson, shooting a rifle. Timmy was excited about it and said,

"I hit the stump, Captain!"

The captain grinned and said, "A boy needs to know how to handle a firearm. Rifle and pistol as well."

Frank jolly said, "Jeremy Deaver is as good with his bow and arrows as any red man ever was!"

Jeremy said, "Timmy, here can shoot a bow might near as good as *I can*. I been teachin him."

The idle chatter continued as Jeremy cooked some deer meat and potatoes. Fall weather would be coming soon, but for now the weather was pleasant. After some visiting and a meal, Captain Lowe asked Jeremy to step over to a secluded spot away from the others. They could hear Buckley, Jolly and Timmy talking and an occasional laugh.

Captain Lowe spread the map out and showed Jeremy where his cabin was. He showed him where the home place of Ben Ewing and his murdered family was located. The map showed the outline of the Ewing holdings. Jeremy looked at the map and said,

"The boy has a good-sized ranch!"

Captain Lowe pointed to a marked water way. He said,

"This is the Salt Fork of the Brazos. Your little stream is a tiny branch of it. If you follow it back about five miles, you'll come to the spot where Timothy was born and where his people were killed. No mater what anyone else thinks they have, as far as squatter's rights, you built your cabin here before whoever put up that shack on the old home site. Jeremy wasn't grasping what Captain Lowe was telling him. Jeremy said,

"Does Timmy still get his father's place?"

Captain Lowe said,

"Of course! Unless *you* claim Squatter's rights for yourself. I believe enough time has passed from the time the place became abandoned till now. Jeremy, you can own this land if you want to claim it."

Jeremy shook his head and said,

"No... No!! The place belongs to the boy. It belongs to Timmy!"

They all took a ride to the burned-out headquarters that afternoon. They found Sneed, Blair and Fisk sitting around on some cut stumps. Greetings were exchanged and there was more than one conversation going on at the same time.

Timmy and Chapo walked through the ruins and it was easy to see it was painful to Timmy. He was remembering things about that awful tragic day. He spotted the graves of his folks and found Jeremy. Timmy was crying but not aloud. Tears were staining his face, the dirty face of a boy who liked to play in the dirt. Timmy grabbed Jeremy's hand and tugged. Deaver was speaking to Randle Sneed but knew he should see what Timmy wanted. He followed Timmy to the graves of Ben Ewing, his wife, two daughters and the other son. Timmy stood looking at the graves and shed more tears. Instinctively, he knew what the graves were.

Just before dark, Bob Dove and B. B. Kelly rode into the yard behind close to seventy head of E 4 cattle. Blair swung the corral gate open and made a sweeping gesture with his hat. The riders were worn out as were their mounts. Sneed shut the gate behind the last of the cattle to go into the corral. Bob Dove was astonished to see this crowd of people here. He looked over at B. B. Kelly as if to say, *'The jig is up'*.

Captain Lowe remembered Bob Dove as the man who tried to pass another boy off as Timothy Ewing. Lowe had a distaste for crooks or anyone trying to beat an honest person out of something. Captain Lowe walked up to Bob Dove still sitting in the saddle. He said,

"Mister? I don't recall your name, but I remember your face. Are you two the ones been living here in this thrown up shack?"

Bob Dove could only nod. He remembered the dressing down he got from the Ranger Captain more than a couple years back. Dove looked over at B. B. Kelly and said,

"We been partnered up for quite a spell. We ain't done nothin wrong. We branded some unbranded calves that was without their mothers."

Captain Lowe said, "Dismount and let's see just how many laws you broke." He went on,

"You branded calves with, I assume, your brand although you don't own any cows? You moved in on a place where no one was living because they were murdered and buried here? You tried to gain ownership of this place by falsely claiming some other child was Timothy Ewing...?"

B. B. Kelly and Bob Dove who once tried to ride the outlaw trail but now were doing well in the cattle business were facing their future. Bob Dove dug the ground with the toe of his boot. He couldn't look Captain Lowe in the eyes. He stood there taking the admonishment he was being dealt. Captain Lowe said,

"I don't believe I have anything on you right now that would warrant hangin you but you're through around here."

Jeremy Deaver spoke up, "Captain? I been thinkin about all this. Timmy becomes the rightful owner of this place. We've hired Frank Jolly, here to run the cow operation and he's gonna need some help with the cattle. We're gonna need a couple ranch hands."

Deaver turned to look at Frank Jolly and back to Bob Dove and his partner. Frank Jolly nodded his approval to Deaver's proposal.

Bob Dove and B. B. Kelly were offered a job. They weighed the other possibilities looming in Captain Lowe's authority and accepted the jobs offered. They both stayed on with the Ewing ranch, earning an honest wage for many years. Bob Dove and B. B. Kelly were persuaded to sell their B reverse B brand to Timothy Ewing, giving him ownership of the calves, the pair had branded. The fee for the brand was adequately fair in exchange for the work the two had done. The brand was never used again after the last of the calves that were branded such.

Captain Lowe and six Texas Rangers along with Frank Jolly went to the Ingraham ranch and several neighboring ranches and collected any and all cattle branded with the E 4 brand. Timmy Ewing had nearly all his father's cattle back with the exception of the calves that had been sold off.

Eventually, a new house was built on the original home site. The cabin that Jeremy Deaver built in the meadow was on the southern end of the Ewing holdings and became a line camp. It was mandatory that it was kept in good order.

Timothy was close to Jeremy Deaver and accepted him as his full partner although Deaver would never accept any wages that were offered. Jeremy Deaver looked after the overall business for his young friend. He would say,

"Timmy, I've got a roof over my head, food — anything I need is paid for. I don't need money and I'm content and happy. I just want you to be successful, honest and fair in all your dealings. You were lost and alone, except for Chapo when you came into my life."

Jeremy Deaver had taught Timothy to read and speak with the use of his Bible. He taught the boy his colors. He taught him how to count and write his number figures. He taught him how to add, subtract and multiply. Jeremy wanted to pass his Bible down to Timothy when he decided to live out his years in the cabin by the meadow, but Timothy encouraged Jeremy to keep it with him because he knew how much comfort that Bible gave Jeremy.

By the time Timothy, or Timmy as he preferred to be called turned sixteen years of age, he was as good with horses and cattle as anyone in his employ. He learned quickly from the men who worked for him. Bob Dove learned that good, honest, hard work paid much better. He rewarded his loyal cow hands by letting them run a small bunch of their own cattle. The B reverse B brand was never used. Dove and Kelly registered the DK brand and remained partners for their lifetime.

Chapo lived to be an old dog and holds a special burial spot with the rest of the family. When Jeremy Deaver became unable to work, he requested to live the remainder of his life in the cabin he'd built at the edge of the meadow.

Timmy found him there one day lying on a buffalo robe under the arbor. He was buried in the family plot as well. Timothy read out of Deaver's Bible at the small service. On his headstone was carved, Jeremy "Dad" Deaver.

The cattle industry in Texas flourished and Timothy Ewing became a wealthy, successful rancher. His E 4 brand was on many head of cattle that went north on the large cattle drives to every major cow town.

Made in the USA
Columbia, SC
03 June 2024